West Fork

West Fork

Tom McKay

ISBN # 978-1-878326-22-5
Published by East Hall Press
Augustana College
Rock Island, Illinois
January, 2014

Printed in the United States of America

Design and format by the staff of East Hall Press:
    Alex Bruozis, Chelsea Fray, Maissie Giacovelli, Robert Hamill,
    Samantha Paddock, Alli Petrassi, Laura Seeber, Rachel Wenc

Faculty Editor: Dr. Karin Youngberg

Cover Art Illustration: Ingrid Kallick

*To all the unknown and unnoted
whose lives create stories of
deep loss and enduring love*

Acknowledgements

The thank you list for bringing this novel to print must begin with the people of East Hall Press at Augustana College. Their commitment to literature from the Quad-City area enriches a region in which many places such as West Fork once served as vibrant centers of community life. Special thanks are due to Karin Youngberg, for her enthusiasm, leadership, and knowledge. Student editors each made contributions to the preparation and design of this book for publication.

Any writer can benefit from honest and open critiques by peers. As a member of a long-standing critique group in Madison, Wisconsin, I received invaluable suggestions and support from Zach Elliott, Teresa Elgezebal, Phyllis DeGioia, Den Adler, Phil Gaustad, Jo Ann Colby, Ingrid Kallick, Gypsy Thomas, and Sarah Moeser.

Ingrid Kallick also contributed her remarkable creative abilities to the book by bringing an image of West Fork to life for the cover art. Debbie Kmetz, my longtime colleague at the State Historical Society of Wisconsin, encouraged me in my efforts to write fiction. Her long list of talents includes exceptional skill as a copy editor which I used to full advantage to make the manuscript presentable to others. Thanks also to Ileana Rodriguez-Silva for Spanish dialogue.

Peg Wallace read the novel in its first draft, and her enjoyment of the story and belief that it should be published helped propel me forward. Jeff Schultz and Pam Durian, educators who started their careers in the era when the story begins, were special readers, and I greatly valued the positive comments I received from each of them. It is perhaps appropriate to note that Pam is a graduate of Augustana College.

Understanding family members provide a source of support unlike any other. My wife, Joyce, encouraged my work and displayed the patience necessary with a writer spending time in fictional worlds. I must also thank my sons, Ben and Chris, whose seasons playing elementary school basketball offered ample opportunities to experience tiny gymnasiums in rural communities.

Finally, the characters created by any writer become real in some sense to that author. While I don't believe I have reached the stage where I have imaginary friends, I do miss the characters when a story ends. So, thank you to Jim and Linda.

Prologue

I didn't plan to stay in West Fork for twenty-seven years. I came to town as an outsider and outsiders didn't stay in West Fork. In fact, outsiders barely slowed down for the small clutch of buildings on either side of State Highway 22. If they took any notice at all of the little western Illinois crossroads, they saw a couple dozen frame houses; all but a few painted white, as if to deny any differences in size or style or age, and a handful of business buildings; wood ones before 1930, mostly cement block after. West Fork was much too small to hold any dreams for an outsider.

I remember asking Linda Bray, "How can a place with only ninety people even call itself a town?" And only a place so small could have a name like West Fork. In a larger place, people would ask, "west fork of what?" In a place so small, everybody in town knows the answer—and nobody else cares.

When I came to West Fork, almost everybody called me Mr. Blair. Of course, my students in the Plum River Elementary School called me Mr. Blair, but so did their parents, and so did Ed Johnson at Ed's Welding Shop, and so did Bill and Margaret Dublin at the West Fork Store, and so did Howard Miller at Miller's Pump Service. Eventually, most people in West Fork came to call me Jim, not my last class of students, but the others, the kids I taught and watched and helped grow up; I became Jim to them and to their parents and to Margaret and to Howard. That happens when you stay in a place for twenty-seven years.

People in town learned to call me Jim, but most of those kids I taught are grown and gone away. Sadly, Ed Johnson and Bill Dublin are also gone. That happens, too, when you stay in a place for twenty-seven years.

1

August 27, 1968

"James Blair?"

Five minutes in my new room, at my new desk, and I had a visitor. A new room, a new desk, and I was a new teacher. I didn't expect a visitor. After all, three days remained before the start of school. I just hoped to move into my room and my desk today. New teachers don't know what to do about visitors.

"James Blair?" the visitor repeated.

"Uh, yeah."

My mind flashed through two years of teacher training at Fenton College. Did we cover greeting visitors? If we did, "uh, yeah" probably wasn't the recommended response, and this greeting seemed to leave the woman at my classroom door very unimpressed. Her effect on me was quite the opposite. It wasn't her appearance. The blue suit and white blouse must have been warm on this August day, and they seemed designed to show as little style as possible. At first glance, her age was just as hard to figure as the style of her clothes or the plain cut of her hair. No, it wasn't her appearance that froze me at my desk. It was her voice. Her tone commanded all the control missing from my awkward "uh, yeah." Just the sound of her voice filled the classroom more naturally than mine.

"My name is Alice Fredericks. I was the teacher at Lone Oak School. My students will be attending your school this year, and I have delivered the appropriate records to Mrs. Edgar this morning."

"I'm pleased to meet you . . ."

"Miss Fredericks," she stated in the same controlled tone despite my uncomfortable pause. "I've spent the last hour reviewing the progress of each of the Lone Oak students with Mrs. Edgar. You will have only Pamela Moore in your seventh- and eighth-grade classroom. Her brother, Eugene, will be in the second grade. I have explained to Mrs. Edgar, as I am sure you will find, that Pamela is an excellent student. She will do well in your class."

I listened to Miss Fredericks' precise report, hoping to project a professional demeanor quite the opposite of the feeling growing within me. Five minutes ago, I felt good about my early morning start at organizing the new classroom. I would be prepared for the students placed in my care three days hence. Now, I met a teacher who already had spent a full hour this morning with Mrs. Edgar just to prepare me for the students taken from her care three months past.

Lone Oak was one of the three country schools that closed and consolidated with the West Fork School to form the new Plum River Elementary School District. The West Fork teachers, Mrs. Anderson and Mrs. Edgar, took positions in the new district. Mrs. Edgar received the appointment as principal in addition to teaching the third and fourth grades. Mrs. Abbott and I were new teachers in the district. I understood that two of the three country school teachers found jobs downstate. Miss Fredericks must have been the third country school teacher.

"Mr. Blair, I have a favor to ask of you."

A subtle shift in Miss Fredericks' voice recaptured my wandering thoughts. Was her change in tone a sign of impatience at my inattention or simply a gentle plea for help from a stranger too young and too inexperienced to be truly thought of as a colleague?

"As you know," she continued, "this school's entry hall has a display case. I have asked Mrs. Edgar to allow me to place an item from the Lone Oak School in the case, but I need some assistance."

"I'd be glad to help."

"Let me explain first," she replied. "Lone Oak School was built in 1893. During the First World War, the district school board voted to donate the school's large brass bell to a scrap drive. Several years later, in 1925, my predecessor, Miss Stillman, began a campaign to replace the bell. She secured enough money through contributions from parents and neighbors to pay for a much smaller bell that served the school until it closed last spring. The bell is of a size to fit in the display case, and Mrs. Edgar has agreed to its placement there. Mr. Bray, a parent of one of my former students, has agreed to take down the bell, but he needs the assistance of another man. I felt it might be appropriate for you to help him."

"Sure," I answered, actually feeling quite unsure. "What would you like me to do?"

"Mr. Bray owns a farm near the school," Miss Fredericks said. "He can take the bell down tomorrow afternoon. If you could be at the Lone Oak School at three-thirty, Mr. Bray will bring all of the necessary tools. Hoping that you would be available to assist him, I took the liberty of writing directions to the school on this paper. I will appreciate your help very much."

August 28, 1968

The road to Lone Oak School rolled over the small rises in an unremark-able Illinois countryside. The gravel strip passed cornfields and fences, pastures and cows, and, at almost regular intervals, communities of A-frame hog houses and their residents. I traveled this ordinary farm road in my very ordinary auto-mobile—a green, 1962 Ford Falcon—a five hundred dollar used car bargain that I tried to reassure myself reflected my bank account more than my personality. At the crest of a ridge slightly higher than the surrounding countryside, I came to Lone Oak School, arriving in a small cloud of gravel dust and with the slight-est aura of self-satisfaction at pulling into the driveway five minutes early for my three-thirty appointment with Miss Fredericks and Mr. Bray.

A single oak tree loomed over the right side of the white frame school build-ing, and a galvanized metal swing set and slide stood to the other side. I walked across the dusty schoolyard and climbed three concrete steps to the front door of the building. The one-room school seemed as plain as the countryside surround-ing it.

The front door of the Lone Oak School led into a small entryway. Opening a second inside door, I saw Miss Fredericks gazing out a tall side window that pre-sented a view of the Illinois farmland reaching toward the horizon. As I stepped into the room, she turned in my direction.

"Good afternoon, Mr. Blair."

"Good afternoon, Miss Fredericks."

Though my greeting was a marked improvement over the previous day's encounter, the look on my face must have revealed my startled reaction at entering a completely empty room.

"You were expecting desks and books and pictures, I imagine," Miss Fredericks said. "When the school closed at the end of May, I arranged all of the records and transferred them to the Plum River District. The school board chose to auction all the furnishings."

"That must have been hard," I said, though hard seemed in no way an adequate word.

Filled with its furnishings, the old schoolroom might have been a soft, nostalgic portrait of an American era almost past. Empty, the room lost all softness. Perhaps Miss Fredericks' memories could paint that portrait again in her mind as she stood near the tall window. All I could see were the blemishes left by brackets and nails that once held shelves and hooks, the scars worn into the floor by rows of school desks, and the forlorn outlines of maps, pictures, and blackboards stripped from the walls. Blemished, worn, forlorn, those were better words for this empty room.

"The auction took place in July. I was summering in Michigan as usual, Mr. Blair."

"Oh, good, uh, I guess." I stumbled over my own awkwardness and uncertainty again. "Uh, Miss Fredericks, could I ask you a favor? I'm used to being called Jim, if, you know, that's okay with you."

"Let's walk outside, Jim," she replied in a quiet, calming voice.

I followed Miss Fredericks down the concrete steps and around to the back of the frame building. She spoke again in a new voice, not far from her precise reporting of yesterday or her calming tone moments earlier, but new, nonetheless. She had a control of language and expression that I realized fell outside my grasp. So often, I had thoughts I could not even translate into conversation, much less indicate with changes in my tone of voice. Were her subtle shifts merely techniques perfected through years as a teacher, or did her voice reveal parts of a personality otherwise held purposely out of view behind the plain clothes and simple hair style?

"This was my favorite time of year," she said. "That little creek down below is the east fork of the Plum River. It curves around this hill and cuts the school off from the Bray's farm across the way. Mr. Bray pastures the land beyond the creek, just like his father did when I came here in 1941. That scrub growth along the creek bottom hides the fences. It even hides a little island in the middle of the creek."

Miss Fredericks' voice cracked almost imperceptibly, and she paused for a moment.

"Every year, before the children started school, I would stand right here and look out across the way. Down the hill you can see the long dry grass, the pods opening on the milkweed, and the scrub willows and sumac along the creek banks. Standing on this spot, there is not a fence in sight. I've tried to imagine the land before white people settled here. Before roads and wires and tractors and windmills. Before my little, white one-room schoolhouse. I always envisioned tall prairie grasses and buffalo in place of our corn and cows."

I nodded at the picture she drew with her words.

"I'll miss that," she said. "No fences to see nor any fences on the imagination."

Miss Fredericks and I gazed in silence down the little hill and across the stream to the pasture land beyond. She had no wish to speak, and no words came to me. Still, I understood that the landscape I had thought so unremarkable could be seen with different eyes.

Did the quiet last only moments, or did it stretch on like Miss Fredericks' imaginary, unfenced prairie? When the sound of a pickup truck rumbling down the gravel road broke the silence, I glanced down at my watch. Somehow, it read ten minutes to four. Miss Fredericks read my thoughts.

"I don't believe that's him. I am afraid I brought you here early. Mr. Bray debated between three-thirty and four o'clock to take down the bell. I must have given you the wrong time."

The mistake seemed very unlike Miss Fredericks. I followed as she motioned back toward the front of the schoolhouse.

"As I mentioned, the land across the creek belongs to the Bray farm," she said. "It has been in that family for many years. The Brays' daughter, Linda, attended this school. She was one of the best pupils I ever taught. She is a veterinary student now, in Laurel, Michigan, at Michigan A&E."

A hint of lightness and a small measure of self-satisfaction moved ever so softly through her words. Miss Fredericks must have brought me here early on purpose. She needed to teach me about Lone Oak School. Maybe she also needed to teach me about this place, a small knoll perched on the rolling prairie. Now, however, the shift in her mood almost reversed the situation. Whatever she had wanted to reveal to me about this place, the place began to reveal her instead. What brought the change into her voice? Why did it rise with the mention of Laurel, Michigan? Did she see herself in the former student who now attended college there?

While her words carried no answers to these questions, the tone I heard began to show me Miss Fredericks. In my classroom yesterday, I couldn't get a fix on her age. Standing next to her schoolhouse today, it seemed clear that Miss Fredericks had to be in her fifties. I guessed fifty-two or fifty-three. And her voice suggested a life with other stories—stories beyond the role of dedicated teacher that she so carefully projected through her clothes and her hair. I began to wonder about that life, but of those stories I would learn no more. The sound of another pickup truck on the gravel road broke through her voice and through my thoughts. With a glance at the distant cloud of gravel dust, Miss Fredericks' voice changed again.

"That should be Mr. Bray," she said.

My eyes followed the dust rising along the road until a bright red Ford pick-up swung into the open schoolyard. As he stepped out of the truck, Donald Bray looked like a farmer, not the old farmers in overalls pulling mud-splattered trailers to the livestock auction, but the picture of the prosperous middle-aged farmer climbing onto a John Deere tractor in a *Life* magazine advertisement.

I judged him to be about my height at six feet or a little more. His short-sleeved shirt revealed thickly muscled arms and a slightly padded stomach. Strength was a better word than fitness to attach to his appearance, but he must have been an athlete when he was young. Only athletes—for that matter, star athletes—ever knew how to roll the bill and form the crown on a baseball cap as perfectly as that of the green and yellow DeKalb seed corn hat he wore. Probably in his late forties now, Mr. Bray walked with a confident stride befitting a man who commanded the modern day prairie landscape. As Donald Bray approached, the new schoolteacher waiting to help him felt none of the confidence so apparent in the experienced farmer. Miss Fredericks made the introductions.

"Mr. Bray, I would like you to meet Jim Blair, the new seventh- and eighth-grade teacher in West Fork."

"It's nice to meet you, Jim," Don Bray nodded.

"It's nice to meet you, sir."

I heard the word *sir* in my own voice although I had no idea where it came from. I doubted that I had spoken the word in four years of college, but it came immediately to my tongue upon meeting Don Bray.

"I brought everything we need," he said. "We should have that thing down in two shakes of a lamb's tail if that bell tower is as sturdy as I think it is. Jim, let's grab that ladder in the back of my truck."

Miss Fredericks walked with us as Don Bray and I, one at each end, carried a heavy wooden extension ladder toward the school. His other hand gripped a large red toolbox, yet he walked, each hand grasping its load, without even a hint of strain. His conversation, directed more toward Miss Fredericks than me, came in an equally unstrained manner.

"My father always said," he started, "that our bell set Lone Oak apart from other schools. Not that many country schools have a bell on top. In Dad's mind, that bell showed people that we believed in our school. I suppose that I got it from him, but I always felt the same way. It's a good thing to save that bell."

It was a simple observation, passed from one generation to the next, but one that would have escaped my notice forever if not for Don Bray's words. The low bell tower squatting on the Lone Oak School roof suddenly stood out. As half-remembered images of other country schools flashed through my mind, few roof lines sported a bell tower. However modest the bell mounted atop Lone Oak School, Don Bray's words held their own clear ring of truth. All communities, even those as small as the clusterings of farm families that had made up the Lone Oak School District, need symbols.

Miss Fredericks understood this symbol, but now I saw something more in the faint smile that played across her face. She wanted me to see that communities have symbols and that good teachers know and understand them. Was this lesson the only reason she asked me to help with the bell, or was it one of a hundred subtle messages she hoped to leave with me through this visit to Lone Oak School? Whatever her reasons, Don Bray's manner destroyed the pretense that he needed much help with the bell. His instructions came clipped and sure.

"Jim, hold this ladder while I climb up and get a rope through those standards. If I put in a double hitch and go up over that center beam, we can lower the bell to the floor with the rope. Grab a five-eighths socket and hand it up."

His instructions made me freeze at the foot of the ladder. I had nodded knowingly at his plan to tie a double hitch—whatever that was. But now, his directions required not a mere nod but real action.

"In the red box," he said.

My ears flushed their own shade of red as I reached for the set of socket wrenches. Of course that's what he wanted. Even my minuscule knowledge of shop tools included socket wrenches in its vocabulary. Twisting one of the small, chrome-plated tools in my fingers, I squinted at the tiny numbers engraved in the metal. His words came before I could decipher the fraction on the socket in my hand.

"No, to the left."

I fumbled in the box then saw the printed key marking each properly placed socket. I picked the tool from the slot marked five-eighths in bold black numbers and started up the ladder toward Don Bray.

"I'll need the handle, too," he said as my foot touched the first rung.

Don Bray's short, clipped phrases from the bell tower conveyed an unmistakable, though perhaps involuntary, expression of surprise. His manner left no doubt that he was a man who knew how to do things. His reaction to my fumblings made it equally clear that he expected the same of other men.

During my conversation with Miss Fredericks behind the Lone Oak School, twenty minutes had passed like five. Working with Don Bray to loosen and lower the small bell turned that equation around. By the time the bell touched the floor and Don descended the ladder, beads of sweat clung to my forehead and moistened my shirt. In Don Bray's world, a man could no doubt earn respect through the sweat of a hard day's work, but the nervous perspiration on my face claimed no such status. Fortunately, Lone Oak School remained Miss Fredericks' world, and her voice quickly redirected the situation away from double-hitch knots and socket wrenches.

"How is Linda?" she asked.

"She called three days ago," Don replied. "She says the feeding study she's working on is finally beginning to show some real results. She talked quite awhile to her mother—longer than usual. Linda says it's nice to have a long conversation in English, but I think she's also getting ready to come home. You know Linda. She's not going to say so."

"When is she due back?" Miss Fredericks asked.

"Early November," he answered.

"Mr. Bray's daughter, Linda, is on an agricultural exchange program from Michigan A&E to Bolivia," Miss Fredericks said, turning slightly toward me. "We are all very proud of her."

"Helen and I both think you deserve part of the credit, Miss Fredericks. Who knows if Linda would have ended up at A&E without your help?"

"I attended Laurel College in the same town as Michigan A&E," Miss Fredericks explained. "I knew Linda had always dreamed of being a veterinarian, and I also knew A&E has one of the country's best veterinary schools. It seemed natural that a student with Linda's abilities should aim for the best. To that end, I did encourage her to investigate A&E, but I have no doubt that she would have found an excellent school with or without my interest."

"Miss Fredericks, you know we still appreciate all you did," Don said. "Being a vet makes a lot of sense for Linda. She's loved the farm ever since she was old enough to walk. Say she finds a guy who wants to farm, he could take over for me at our place someday. As a vet, she'd still be able to work part time when they start a family."

All the talk about Linda Bray's talent in school had deflected attention away from my lack of talent with things mechanical. Although we had never met, I felt grateful that the interest in her future had offered relief from my present predicament. As Don and I loaded the old school bell into the back of his truck, I ruefully noted that I should meet her sometime to give proper thanks in person.

October 19, 1968

I looked forward to Saturday mornings. They were my time—no papers to grade, no lessons to plan, no students to quiet, no daily dose of Mrs. Edgar checking up on any or all of the above. Mrs. Edgar particularly valued a quiet classroom. By the end of a week, I needed my time.

I had not gone to college to become a teacher, but I had gone to college to become something. If nothing else, the cost of four years in college convinced me of the need to become something. Almost every penny I ever earned and many more from my parents, probably more than they could afford, went into my college education. Sometime in my junior year, I told my parents that teachers were something the world would always need. I told myself that the draft deferment given to most men with teaching jobs was not an important part of my decision. I convinced my family of my reason for choosing teaching more thoroughly than I convinced myself.

If I had entered my first week as an educator unconvinced of my commitment to teaching, I concluded the week with the certain knowledge that I had used up every idea I had for the classroom in five days. Since that first week, I confronted the same terror each Sunday night. What would I do, what could I do, with the kids this week? But today was Saturday, my time.

Like most Saturday mornings, I headed over to the West Fork Store. In West

Fork, no one could go downtown. A handful of businesses sprinkled together with some houses at a country crossroads simply constituted town—all of town. I lived in a tiny house that originally had not been a house at all.

The place I rented at the back corner of the Mitchell property served until twenty years ago as Dr. Mitchell's medical office. His only daughter still lived in the big white house over the grape arbor, past the lilac hedge, and through the flower garden. The plantings stretched across the three lots that formed the Mitchell property and created boundaries between my place and the big house that were as distinct as the boundaries that being the doctor's daughter placed between Irene Mitchell and the rest of the town.

Irene worked as a clerk in one of the two dress shops in Spenceville, fifteen miles away. Her store was the "better" shop, of course. People told me that Dr. Mitchell closed out his practice in the late 1940s and passed away only a few months later. Irene remained "the doctor's daughter" although for years the only medical man in West Fork had been Doc Shelby. He had his veterinary clinic on the county road just south of the highway.

My house faced a side street, a half-block north of Highway 22. At the corner on the highway, Hazel Anderson kept the post office in one room of her house. Next to her came Howard Miller's Pump Service, then the West Fork Fire Station. Across the highway stood the West Fork Store, a small frame building with a short false front. In the next block, Ed's Welding Shop and the pole shed where Wayne Mitton kept his excavating equipment sat opposite Betty's Kut and Kurl beauty salon and two white frame houses. In this tiny knot of businesses, only the West Fork Store presented much likelihood of more than one car parked in front at any given time. This Saturday morning, I recognized Doc Shelby's Mercury and Wayne Mitton's pickup pulled in next to the store.

The mid-October morning sparkled with a warm sun in a bright blue sky. On a day like this, you could even believe that the weather in western Illinois could surround you with a comfortable glow for at least another month, possibly more. Who says nature doesn't lie? It was almost certain that a cold, biting wind would howl down this road by Halloween night; but today, the inside door of the West Fork Store stood open to welcome in the warm, fresh air. As I reached for the screen door, nothing could have been more fitting than the embossed metal bar across the middle advertising Sunny Day Bread.

A customer of the West Fork Store entered not so much a place to shop as a three-dimensional statement of ordinary, everyday tastes and needs. Sections of

14

second-hand shelving displayed boxes, bottles, and cans. Fruit: peaches, applesauce, and fruit cocktail. No apricots—too expensive. No cranberries—too seasonal. Certainly, no Mandarin oranges—too exotic. Soup: tomato, vegetable beef, chicken noodle, and cream of mushroom. Likely as not, few local people ever thought of sitting down to a bowl of cream of mushroom soup for lunch, but just about every casserole recipe in the Methodist Church cookbook called for a can of mushroom soup at some point. Cereal: corn flakes and bran flakes. Detergent: two brands; hand soap: three. And so it went all the way to the small rack of hardware. Screwdrivers: two sizes of regular, one Phillips-head.

Shelves filled with these reliable, regular sellers occupied the right-hand two-thirds of the West Fork Store. On the left-hand side of the store stood the counter, a small meat case, two used dinette tables, and an eclectic mixture of chrome and vinyl kitchen chairs. Bill and Margaret Dublin, the store's owners, enjoyed auctions and apparently stayed perpetually on the trail of extra kitchen chairs to replace the well-worn veterans that served the coffee crowd in the West Fork Store. Margaret kept a pot of coffee brewing all day and opened two boxes of Jumping Johnny Donuts, powdered and chocolate, every morning.

At lunchtime on weekdays, she sliced cold cuts and cheese from the meat case and made sandwiches for anyone who knew to ask. Most days found a county road crew or maybe a couple of telephone linemen arrayed around the dinette tables with bags of potato chips, packages of cupcakes, bottles of pop, and Margaret's handmade sandwiches piled in front of them. A hungry guy could eat for two bucks, easy. Saturday's dinette crew mostly lounged over coffee and donuts, a pattern I had grown accustomed to in little more than a month in town.

"Good morning, Mr. Blair. What will you have?"

Margaret Dublin still called me Mr. Blair. I had requested Jim, but Margaret, though as friendly as anyone I had met, held to Mr. Blair as a more proper greeting for the new schoolteacher.

"A cup of coffee and a chocolate donut, please."

I doubted that anyone had ever jumped for a chocolate Jumping Johnny Donut. The dark coating came much closer to sweet, brown wax than anything that should be called chocolate. Even so, I always ordered chocolate. My problem was that I could never figure out a way to eat the powdered sugar donuts without leaving a mess on the dinette table. Ed Johnson regularly decorated his spot with powdered sugar then picked the fine white powder off the table with a moistened index finger, keeping a steady rhythm from mouth to table and back. Somehow, this seemed improper etiquette for my standing in the community as an educator. Leaving a covering of powdered sugar at my place struck me as even less polite than Ed's solution. To protect the dignity of my position, I always chose the chocolate.

"Good morning, Jim. Sit down."

Doc Shelby's comfortable greeting felt good. I had met Doc my first week in town, one of numerous introductions to the community's leaders during those first seven days. Unlike most of the people I met, Doc Shelby sensed, even before I spoke, the awkward self-consciousness of a young teacher searching for the right things to say. Maybe thirty years of tending to the ills and soothing the fears of animals that could not speak at all let Doc sense my feelings through just a handshake or the look in my eyes.

"Jim, do you know Wayne Mitton?" Doc asked.

"We met a couple of weeks ago," I answered with a nod to both Doc and Wayne.

"I just wanted to be sure you two knew each other," Doc said in his easy manner, as if everybody within ten miles didn't already know who belonged to the one new face in West Fork.

A pretty steady thump of the screen door punctuated Saturday mornings in the West Fork Store. I barely sat down before Howard Miller and another man joined us at the table. Each held a cup of coffee and a donut—one chocolate, one sugared. Doc did the honors on the introductions, and I learned that the second man was Bill Carey, a farmer "about five-and-a-half miles out on the county highway" as Howard Miller put it. Mr. Miller had just replaced a "three-sixteenths bearing in an eight-year-old pump Bill has on his 500-gallon stock tank."

I marveled at Howard Miller. A friendly and gregarious man, Howard spoke in numbers. He didn't discuss the world, he sized it up and described it—described it in feet and miles and hours and pounds and points and electrical wattages and anything else he could put to a number. I had his son Andy as one of my eighth-graders. I liked Andy and I liked Howard, though as his son's teacher I figured to remain Mr. Blair to him, and he Mr. Miller to me, for some time to come.

"You working today, Wayne?" Howard asked between bites of his donut.

"I have to dig the grave for Mrs. Elkins' funeral," Wayne answered. "The service is on Monday. I'll go up and dig it yet this morning. I don't like to take the tractor in too early when there's been a heavy dew. Tears the grass up. I like everything neat as I can make it for a funeral. People have too much on their minds to have to see a mess."

It hadn't taken me long to learn that this was Wayne Mitton, always concerned about other people, and this was West Fork, always proud of its work.

"If you wait two or three hours, I'll bet it helps a hundred percent on a day like this," Howard responded.

"Darn right," Wayne said.

That, too, was Wayne. If Howard always spoke in numbers, Wayne never used the word *yes*. Wayne Mitton seemed to know only one way to give an affirmative answer, "darn right."

"How about you, Howard?" Wayne asked. "You been busy?"

"I'd say it's the busiest fall for six or seven years. I must've put three hundred fifty miles on my truck in one week. Tuesday, I started at six-thirty and didn't finish up until eight o'clock that night. I had five service calls and ran up twice to Saukdale for parts. There's times I don't have to hunt up parts twice in three months."

"You better be careful, Howard," Bill Carey laughed. "You'll ruin your reputation for having a part in that storage room of yours for every pump ever made. Hell, I'm afraid to go back there by myself when I'm looking for you. A guy might get buried in that junk and never come out."

"Well, I'll tell you what," Howard shot back. "That might look like a mess to you, but it's 250-square-feet of junk that got the pump on your 500-gallon tank back up and running in about an hour-and-a-half. What do you think, Wayne? Farmers always got an opinion, but if it wasn't for three guys like you and me and Doc, fifty percent of 'em would go out of business in about two weeks."

"Darn right," Wayne said. "Probably go out owing us money to boot."

The four men laughed good-naturedly. I smiled but held myself to just a smile. In Howard Miller's off-hand joke, three guys completed the circle of essential services to the farmers. I held a different position and not one that allowed laughing along with a joke about farmers.

"Jim, I hear you're going to be busy coaching basketball this year," Doc said. "It's a great thing with the new school, the kids being able to have a team."

"Darn right," Wayne agreed.

"We've had a school in this town for almost ninety years, and this will be the first real sports team," said Howard.

"Don't you remember the county exercises we had at the end of school when we were kids?" Wayne asked. "We had races and ball throwing contests and all kinds of things."

"Remember! I threw a baseball two hundred and fifteen feet when I was in sixth grade. Got second place. Still, one day of exercises, that's not the same as a real team that plays fifteen or twenty games."

"Andy play basketball?" Bill Carey asked Howard.

"I'll tell you what. We must have bought that kid ten pairs of blue jeans in the last six months. He's grown a good five or six inches this year. He'll be out for the team."

"We can use that height, Mr. Miller," I said. "Mrs. Edgar says even though our team is sixth, seventh and eighth graders, we have to play the eighth-grade teams from the bigger schools like Saukdale and Spenceville."

"That doesn't sound real fair," Bill Carey said.

"I guess it's a rule," I answered. "If you have any eighth graders at all, you have to play the eighth-grade teams."

I tried to sound as self-assured as possible in my answer. Inside I knew Bill Carey's concern about fairness couldn't match my anxiety at the thought of trying to hold our own against eighth-grade teams from bigger schools. I had no idea how good our players would be, but I knew their coach lacked any knowledge whatsoever about organizing a basketball team. Mrs. Edgar assigned me to coach the team because I was the only male teacher. Informal games of "pickup" and "horse" served as my only qualifications—other than a Y-chromosome—to coach basketball.

"That's the way this country is anymore," Bill Carey said. "They make all kinds of rules about the little things, but we aren't worth a damn about keeping the big things under control. Anybody see that California protest on the news last night? That's all you see on TV anymore. A bunch of long-haired bums carrying signs against the war."

Just that suddenly it appeared. One minute, five men laughed and joked over strong coffee and bland donuts in a friendly corner of Bill and Margaret Dublin's little store in a tiny town on the western Illinois prairie. The next minute Vietnam, a country of meandering rivers, thick jungles, and a war more twisted and tangled than any of its rivers or jungles, came crashing into the conversation from half a world away. Now, no strong coffee, no bland donuts, no homey dinette table, no clear autumn morning could make it go away.

"I saw about five minutes of it," Howard said with his voice tensing. "A bunch of idiots getting their faces on a million TV sets while good young men go fight a war for 'em. I'd take a couple thousand of those draft-dodgers and lock them up for twenty years. That would end it in about one week. Don't you think, Wayne?"

Wayne Mitton shifted slightly in his chair and fumbled with the handle of his coffee cup. The eyes around the table turned to him as he took a drink of black coffee. His eyes followed the cup as he placed it down again.

"I'll say this much," Wayne finally said without looking up. "I sure hate to see what's going on in this country right now."

A silence of thoughts unspoken spread across the table. I felt my ears turn hot and red as I wondered if any of the thoughts were about me. At twenty-two, with a deferment for teaching, where did I fit in Howard Miller's universe of good young men and draft-dodgers? How did I rate on Bill Carey's scale of fairness? Why was Doc Shelby so quiet? With a few quick sips of coffee and a vague excuse about grading papers, I slipped through the screen door of the West Fork Store and out into the peaceful autumn morning.

November 11, 1968

The double doors of the Plum River Elementary School flew open with a force equal to fifteen first graders charging out to recess—except it was seven o'clock, seven in the evening. The head that banged into my chest, rather than my belt buckle, confirmed that the attempt to knock the school doors off their hinges came from someone other than a first grader.

"Sorry," snapped a woman's voice.

She didn't sound sorry. She sounded annoyed. And she looked angry, almost fierce. Her coat swarmed around her, unzipped against the stinging cold of a nasty November wind. Nature's last warm echoes of summer had passed by two weeks ago. Now, this human storm had swept into me, then away, as well. My startled senses picked up only a few of her features. Fair skin, short hair, pale blue eyes with deep black pupils. The eyes I would remember. Even in our brief encounter, I could see in her eyes feelings so intense that they left my own emotions unsettled.

With an involuntary shake of my head, I regathered my thoughts. Actually, the brief encounter—better yet collision—knocked some of the nervousness out of me. If the world needed a good physiological study of nervousness, I could volunteer. After all, nervousness should start in the head and work its way down to the stomach. I felt sure mine flowed in the opposite direction. If a scientist could prove that nerves actually started in the stomach and not in the brain, maybe he could experiment with the effects of someone's head ramming into your chest as a way to interrupt the flow. Anyway, I suddenly felt a little better, and I had been nervous about tonight's Veterans' Day dinner since my alarm clock rang this morning.

The dinner really required very little of me. All I had to do was show up and act like a teacher. After three months, I usually managed that with children, but their parents presented an entirely different problem. Maybe I still felt like a kid myself. Maybe I thought all adults could see through the teacher's personality that I put on each morning. The parents made me nervous. To top that off, the first public display of my teacher's judgement would happen tonight. The Veterans' Day dinner committee had asked me to choose an eighth-grade boy to lead the Pledge of Allegiance.

Five boys and four girls comprised the Plum River Elementary School eighth-grade class. From that group, no one stood out less than Jeff Larson. Jeff never caused trouble and never excelled. Jeff stood taller than two boys and shorter than two others. He weighed less than three and more than one. Nobody ever picked Jeff first for a team. The same held true for being chosen last. As I considered a choice to lead the pledge, I contemplated the possibility that Jeff Larson might spend his whole life without ever being set apart from the group. I couldn't think of a better reason to select a student for the pledge, so I chose Jeff. I think he was happy. Jeff's feelings didn't stand out much, either.

Entering the gymnasium, I hoped for the security of finding Doc Shelby to sit with and silently thanked my good fortune when I saw an empty chair next to him at the end of a table. My strategic location promised to limit most of the evening's conversation to Doc and Betty and Bob Lingafelder seated across the table. Betty chatted a mile a minute, an asset, no doubt, at Betty's Kut and Kurl. Bob, her husband, spoke very little, but then Betty didn't leave much room in a conversation. Bob mostly smiled a contented smile and nodded. I figured to do the same for the evening. I barely squeezed in a greeting to the Lingafelders and Doc before Betty sped into her first subject for the night.

"Say, Doc, I thought I saw Linda Bray here a minute ago."

"She is back from Bolivia . . ."

"She working for you again?" Betty asked before Doc could finish his thought.

"No, no, she'll be back in school at the first of the year," Doc said. "She stopped by a couple of days ago, but I think a month's break from worrying about the health of cows will do her good right now."

"Well, I wonder where she is. I know she was here," Betty stated definitively. "She wouldn't leave. Not with her dad and all. You know, Don's Navy record being what it was."

The mention of the Navy surprised me. Don Bray's bearing spoke of a man who had been in the service, but western Illinois placed a person just about as far away from an ocean as you could get in this country. To me, farmers and sailors seemed an incongruous mix. I turned the thought one way and perceived a straight and narrow Midwestern boy seeking his one chance for a strange new adventure. Still, turning the thought around, the vast, open ocean could be almost in harmony with the broad, flat lands of the prairie.

"Do you know her, Mr. Blair?"

Betty's question caught me in mid-thought.

"Know who?" I said.

"Linda Bray. I just wondered if you'd seen her. She should be here. Do you know her?"

"Uh, no, I don't," I said, realizing in the same instant that, like Betty, I too had seen Linda Bray. I had seen her too late to avoid colliding with her, but I felt certain it was her and equally certain that I should not share the circumstances with our table.

"Well, I just don't know," Betty concluded as she launched into a consideration of her next topic—who made the different jello salads cut into square servings at each of our places.

Betty expressed certainty that my lime jello with crushed pineapple and bits of celery came from Hazel Anderson. According to Betty, nobody else put pineapple and celery together. I couldn't tell from Betty's tone whether that was good or bad. Doc had lemon with pears and a dollop of mayonnaise on top—Mary Henry's trademark, according to Betty. Unfortunately, the orange jello with shredded carrots at Betty's place could have come from almost anyone, and Bob had already eaten most of his jello. I guess etiquette forbid discussing the creator of a jello salad that had been reduced to a few smears on a plate. Though Bob had continued to eat throughout Betty's jello commentary, the introduction of Pastor Newberry to say grace brought Bob's fork to a halt.

On the heels of a smattering of "amens," the members of the Methodist Church Ladies Aid Society began the procession of white, ironstone bowls and platters to the tables: round bowls of mashed potatoes, soup bowls pressed into service as gravy boats, oblong platters of Swiss steak, and bowls for both the coleslaw and corn. With confidence and considerable dispatch, the church women served up the classic small town meal, if anything in West Fork could be called classic. That was a question. Maybe the word *classic* fit anything in West Fork about as well as the term *down home* fit anything in New York or Chicago. In West Fork, Swiss steak, mashed potatoes and gravy, corn, rolls and butter, coleslaw, and jello salad constituted not a classic meal, but a tried and true one.

Although people in West Fork often spoke of food and fellowship together, the two held a consecutive rather than simultaneous relationship to each other. The friends and neighbors who filled the small gymnasium enjoyed their food with relatively few words and in relatively short order. Short enough, in fact, that I found no opportunity to become nervous again about the Pledge of Allegiance.

I had not noticed Don Bray moving toward the podium. Of course, there was no need to keep track of such things at our table. We had Betty seated with us for that. As the West Fork area's most decorated World War II veteran made his way forward, I could hear Betty whisper to Bob.

"See, Linda isn't here. There's Helen and the empty place next to her is Don's. I tell you, something's going on. I'm sure Linda was here before."

"Maybe she got sick," Bob answered in an obvious and atypical attempt to end his wife's conversation.

While the content of Bob's response would hardly have stilled Betty, the volume worked wonders. She may have mastered the small town whisper, but Bob lacked such subtleties. As several heads turned in our direction, Betty uttered a quick "shh" and pursed her own lips firmly.

"I want to welcome all of you here tonight to our annual Veterans' Day dinner," Don Bray announced. "I think we should show our appreciation to the ladies for all the fine food we just enjoyed."

A burst of applause rose then subsided in an almost ritual rhythm. Don Bray glanced quickly at the index card in his left hand.

"Now, to start our program, Jeff Larson of Mr. Blair's eighth-grade class will lead us in the Pledge of Allegiance to the flag."

The unexpected sound of my name caught me off guard, as did the sudden beads of perspiration on my forehead. Jeff walked with a stride of youthful determination to Don Bray's side and faced the flag. Hand on heart, without hesitation, he began "I pledge allegiance" and the room joined in as one "to the flag of the United States of America."

How many times had I heard those words? How many times had I repeated them? In all these hundreds of Pledges of Allegiance, I had never seen a smile as big as the one on Jeff's face, never felt a smile as large as the one I wore, and certainly never witnessed parents any more proud than Jeff Larson's mother and father.

January 7, 1969

The students, the parents, the school board, and just about everybody else in the Plum River School District had waited for this day. The smell of popcorn and hot dogs, sold by the PTA, drifted out of the service kitchen at one end of the gym. Strung out along the north wall of the building, three rows of bleachers held the contingent of loyal fans. In one corner of the gymnasium, Mrs. Edgar's blue and gold clad, five-girl cheerleading squad clapped their hands in rhythm. Across the way, twelve boys—three from the eighth grade, four seventh graders, four sixth graders, and Billy Kimball from the fifth grade—clustered around me as I knelt on the linoleum tile gym floor giving my timeout instructions. The Plum River Rangers were setting up their last play of the first-ever basketball game in the new gym.

"All right, listen up you guys. I want to get one more play in, and let's try to score another basket," I said earnestly.

Twenty feet to our left, the eighth-grade team from Spenceville Junior High School lounged around their coach, probably perplexed by the need for this last second strategy. Even my kids must have wondered why I called a timeout with ten seconds left in the game on the losing end of a forty-four to six score, but I had three sixth graders who had been at the scorekeeper's table for almost two minutes waiting for a break in play to enter the game. From the first minute of the contest, the Spenceville team proved that our five starters had no chance to hold their own, and as I tried to use our reserves, things only got worse, much worse. We had practiced twice during the week, but the game demonstrated with embarrassing clarity just how overmatched and unprepared the Plum River Rangers were.

As bad as the numbers looked hanging from the scorekeeper's table, now I felt even more embarrassed that I had let time slip away with three kids playing less than a minute in the entire game. I knew why I called a timeout.

"Bob, I want you to take the ball out and pass it in to Billy. Andy, set up right next to the free throw line on this side. Okay, Joe and Kenny, you guys stand on opposite sides of the lane down by the basket. Get ready to rebound. If you get a rebound, shoot it. Billy, when the ball comes in to you, dribble toward Andy and pass it to him. Bob, you go right down to the base line as soon as you pass the ball in. Now Andy, if Bob is open, pass the ball to him. Bob, you shoot right away. Andy, if you can't pass to Bob, turn around and take the shot yourself. Everybody understand?"

Five nodding heads in the huddle confirmed that they understood our last play. Unfortunately, five pairs of questioning eyes seemed to say otherwise. A shrill squeal from the scorekeeper's whistle took the issue out of my hands and onto the basketball floor with my five players. The five kids revealed as much as the scoreboard about the level of advancement of the Plum River basketball program.

Andy Miller, our biggest and best player, had scored four points in the game. To Kenny, Joe, and Bob, three sixth-grade reserves, basketball presented mostly a mystery—a game full of plays, rules, and nuances well beyond their simple understanding that you throw a ball through a hoop. Of the three, Bob was the smallest and least athletic, with none of the ball handling skills to play the guard position befitting his size.

Still, Bob could follow directions, and he could shoot. As the last two minutes wound down with the three reserves waiting at the scorekeeper's table, I had watched the anxious look in Bob's eyes, in particular, as he kneeled down, hoping against hope for a chance just to be on the floor again. Now, if Billy and Andy managed to get him the ball, Bob could at least take a shot.

Billy Kimball, a fifth grader, stepped back out on the floor as our fifth player and key ballhandler. His presence summed up our team's unfortunate situation as well as anything. Not that Billy wasn't special. Billy Kimball seemed to have a head start on growing up. He stood as tall as kids a year or two older, played basketball with the intensity of a high school all-stater, and spoke with the self-assurance of an adult. Billy Kimball already knew what he wanted to do with his life. As sure as the sun came up in the morning, Billy knew he would run his family's farm one day.

It required only one meeting with Art Kimball, his father, to understand the source of Billy's intensity and assuredness. When Jerry Peterson, our best eighth-grade guard broke his leg falling off a farm wagon, almost everybody in town suggested adding Billy to the sixth, seventh, and eighth graders on the team. I did, but all of his intensity, self-assurance, and support in town couldn't change the fact that Billy was a fifth grader. Though our best guard, he proved no match for players three years older on Spenceville's team.

The referee's signal pulled me back from my thoughts about Billy. Hesitantly, Bob Martin inbounded the basketball. With two quick, decisive dribbles, Billy moved toward Andy. Almost as quickly, two passes moved the ball from Billy to Andy and back to Bob who had found his place at the base line.

In those few short moments, five boys in Plum River Ranger uniforms looked like a basketball team. The movement of the ball, in exact sequence with the plan, seemed to interrupt the sound filling the gymnasium and suspend the time that had to be moving on the clock. How many seconds did remain? In a sudden rush, time regained its normal pace, the gymnasium rang again with screams and cheers, and the ball arched out of Bob's hands. It dropped gently through the net as the game ended. Final score: Spenceville 44 – Plum River 8.

Out on the floor, Bob Martin's face registered equal parts of pleasure and surprise that he had scored a basket. My expression surely conveyed only surprise. Not surprise that Bob made a shot but amazement that I designed a play and it actually worked. Maybe I could, even should, be something more as a coach than simply the only male teacher at Plum River Elementary School. As I carried a canvas bag of basketballs toward the school's storage room, I acknowledged the greetings from a home crowd in remarkably good spirits.

"Good effort," Doc Shelby said.

"Bob made a good shot, didn't he, Mr. Blair?"

"He sure did," I acknowledged to one of the cheerleaders.

As Don Bray walked by and nodded, I heard Howard Miller's familiar voice behind me.

"Wait two or three games and I'll bet we're the ones puttin' forty on the scoreboard. I know Andy can score three times as many points as he did today. All five of our starters can shoot, and Bob showed you can get some help from those six kids on the bench. One or two baskets a game from that group would be all you need."

"Thanks, Howard. We'll do our best." They were perfunctory words, yet somehow, I knew that I meant them.

June 9, 1969

    The driver's side visor of my old, green Falcon drooped awkwardly as I turned it down against the bright morning sun streaming through my windshield. I headed east down a sandy yellow stretch of gravel road to pick up my new rider. Doc Shelby had suggested the arrangement, and this detour two miles off the highway and back again meant getting out of bed ten minutes earlier to make it to my job in Saukdale. Still, I figured the company on the twenty-five mile drive each morning and afternoon would make it worth the effort.

    In three days at Saukdale Metal Products, I had already grown bored with the straight stretch of highway and the plain farm fields that lined the way from West Fork to the county seat. With no radio in the old Falcon to break the silence, the thought of someone to talk to held a surprising amount of appeal given my usual hesitance about meeting people. I looked forward to some company even though I knew, at first, I would feel as awkward as my drooping sun visor.

    That sense of awkwardness took me to Saukdale in search of summer employment in the first place. I knew I needed a summer job to supplement my first-year teacher's salary, but I didn't know the prevailing public opinion about appropriate part-time positions for teachers. Nine months in West Fork had provided enough experience to guess that talk of a teacher stacking hay bales and cleaning barn stalls might offend the sense of propriety and dignity that the community attached to my position in the Plum River School. I decided to look for summer work in Saukdale. It seemed large enough, at thirty thousand people, and far enough away to lend some sense of anonymity to any job I might find.

Cresting a small rise, I pulled into the driveway of a picture postcard farm. Beds of orange day lilies and a clump of irises covered the foundation along one side of the large, white two-story farmhouse. Down the back walk, a row of peony plants, neatly trimmed of the blossoms that had gone by at least a week ago, separated the clothesline from the rest of the backyard. At the end of the walk, the maroon trumpets of a carefully trained honeysuckle adorned a white trellis attached to the garage. Farther down the driveway loomed a large red barn, with a fresh coat of paint, and an array of well-maintained outbuildings.

My past summers had included a whole range of jobs to pay for college, from dishwasher in an all-night pancake house to stock boy in a variety store to member of the seasonal maintenance crew for a county park back home. In nine summers of work, I had found half-a-dozen jobs, but I suddenly realized that I had walked to each one of them. I had never driven to work and, obviously, never shared a ride.

What was the etiquette for picking up a rider? It seemed too early in the morning to blow my horn. Should I get out and go to the door? Was picking up a rider a front or back door call?

My fleeting panic evaporated as quickly as the questions had formed. As I came to a complete stop, a young woman with short brown hair stepped from the porch that wrapped around the front corner of the farmhouse. She cut directly across the thick, green lawn and walked briskly to the car. With far more assurance than I felt at that moment, she opened the car door and leaned in. Her straight brown hair, turned under at the ends, framed a pretty face with small features and a faint, noncommittal smile playing across her lips. Everything about her said "cute," except for her eyes, pale blue eyes with piercing black pupils.

"Hi, I'm Linda Bray."

"I'm Jim Blair, nice to meet you."

The closing of the car door punctuated our first formal meeting, but the flying open of the front doors of the Plum River Elementary School had placed an exclamation point on my first encounter with Linda Bray. Beside me sat the angry young woman who stormed past me—almost through me—seven months ago at the Veterans' Day dinner. I looked tentatively into those piercing eyes. They showed not a glimmer of recognition.

"I appreciate the ride this summer. It wasn't my idea to work in Saukdale. I wanted to work with Doc Shelby again, but he said a summer at the pet clinic would do me good, give me experience. He set it all up, but, I mean, dogs and cats. I'm studying to be a livestock veterinarian, not some pet doctor. Doc says it's good experience but, geez, dogs and cats. I hate cats."

Her words tumbled out as fast as that door had flown open last November, but they carried more a sense of exasperation than anger. Linda Bray wanted me to know, probably wanted everyone to know, that the pet clinic was not her idea. In rapid-fire fashion, she marked her territory.

"I don't know much about veterinary work," I replied weakly, still lost in my thoughts of company for the ride to Saukdale. Those thoughts had not anticipated her torrent of words.

"Well, I don't know enough about it either," she stated. "So, if I have to spend the whole summer with dogs, cats and parakeets, I don't want to waste the time it takes to drive back and forth to Saukdale. I brought some reading to do in the car if that's okay with you."

"Oh, I don't mind," I said.

I did mind, of course, as I watched her pull out a hardcover text with the intriguing title *Bovine Digestive System Infections*. She didn't want to waste time on the drive. Well, maybe my company was a waste of her time. I certainly couldn't tell her anything about the intestines of sick cows.

I looked at my new rider more carefully. If I was a waste of her time, she wasn't the final word on God's gift to men, either. My first impression told me she had a pretty face. Upon closer inspection, "pleasant," not "pretty," seemed a perfectly adequate description. Nor was her figure anything to write home about. In fact, flat-chested summed up the situation just fine.

I often missed having a radio in my car, and now I wished for one just to intrude on my smug new rider already immersed in her book. Instead, I had only a straight piece of highway and thoughts of my job at Saukdale Metal Products to occupy myself. Those thoughts brought me little joy.

Saukdale Metal Products started in the business of making metal grain scoops eighty-eight years ago, and today, they still manufactured more metal grain scoops than anybody in the country. Of course, not many people used hand grain scoops anymore. Farmers had been turning to more efficient feeding systems for years, and for years the company had added new products—snow shovels, measuring spoons, and dustpans.

Oh, those dustpans! My first two days, I worked on batches of measuring spoons, but yesterday we started a run of dustpans on handles. At Saukdale Metal Products, dustpans on handles were an assembler's headache and a handler's nightmare. I worked as a handler, a handler with two days experience.

Each day, I reported to the assembly room in the main Saukdale Metal Products factory, a fifty-year-old brick building with three large bays. The assembly room occupied the south bay. On one side of the bay, assemblers, nearly all middle-aged farm wives, stood at long work tables next to large banks of windows on the exterior wall. Parts bins lined the interior wall on the opposite side of the bay. Handlers ferried the proper parts across the room to the work tables, one handler to three assemblers.

Monday, I filled and carried trays of spoons, four sizes per set of measuring spoons, two dozen of each size on a tray. For every six trays, I also delivered a bag of wire rings and a pack of paper labels. Each of the women assemblers threaded four different sized spoons onto a ring and wrapped the set in a paper label almost like a cigar band. Each pack of labels carried its own brand name—one label for a hardware chain, another for a kitchen appliance manufacturer, and a third for a variety store.

Assemblers created spoon sets by the gross, and all were identical except for the paper labels designed to convince some homemaker loyal to her electric mixer to buy that set of spoons rather than a store brand in the gadget aisle down at the supermarket. Other than tired feet and a vague discomfort that my mother had probably paid too much for the measuring spoons she bought with her Easy Life pressure cooker, my first two days at SMP passed without undue strain.

Dustpans on handles changed everything and left my comfortable pace of work shattered. In principle, the task of delivering parts to assemblers remained the same. Each assembler required a stack of metal dustpans, a bundle of wooden handles, a batch of wires, and a pack of decals. Blue dustpans and white decals marked one brand of dustpans on handles. Black decals on red dustpans denoted another. In practice, the heavy gauge, V-shaped wires that attached the dustpans to their handles created a job almost too miserable to imagine. If there are factories in hell, they probably make dustpans on handles.

Loose dustpans stacked easily from a pallet box, and wooden handles arrived in bundles from a turning factory. But the damn wires! They came into the assembly room in tall cardboard barrels, straight from a local plating shop. Each barrel held several hundred V-shaped wires, twice as heavy as a coat hanger and, so it seemed, ten times more tangled than the worst jumble of hangers ever encountered. The blunt ends of the wires quickly wore through a set of cloth gloves, leaving the hands inside crisscrossed with nicks, scrapes, and scratches. Yet the pace of work allowed no margin for caution as each handler struggled to untangle wires fast enough to keep his three assemblers supplied. Yesterday, the assemblers I served too often stood at their table with handles screwed into dustpans waiting for my delivery of wires to clip into place. Assemblers were paid piecework. I tested their patience yesterday. I could expect no more understanding or sympathy today.

"My turn is up on the left."

"Huh?" I said, rousing out of the thoughts that had transformed my apprehensions of a difficult day ahead into expectations of a truly dismal one.

"We have to turn on McCoy Road."

We had reached the edge of town, and I turned the Falcon left, bringing it to a stop two blocks later in front of Griffin's Pet Hospital.

"I'll pick you up at ten after four."

"Okay," Linda said, opening the car door. "Have a nice day."

In my mind that possibility had already vanished into the pages of *Bovine Digestive System Infections* and thoughts of dustpans on handles.

June 23, 1969

"Hard day?" Linda asked as she settled into the front seat of my car.

"More dustpans on handles," I said.

That was all I needed to say. Two-and-a-half weeks had allowed me to master wrestling with tangles of dustpan wires well enough to keep pace with my assemblers, but a full day still left my body tired and my hands tattered.

The past two weeks had seen another, more pleasant, development. Linda's veterinary books gradually disappeared, and conversation, rather than scholarship, filled the daily trek from West Fork to Saukdale and back.

"Are those dustpans the only thing your company makes?"

"No, it's just that the summer work's mostly on extra production for special orders. These are to ship for Christmas. The women who work there every summer say we'll do snow shovels next. I guess stores always have a rush on snow shovels during the first week in January. The women say that's when men get tired of using the beat-up, old snow shovels from last year. Who knows?"

"And you said the dustpans are for Christmas?"

"Yeah, you know, with the handles on them and everything, they're a specialty item."

"Who would give somebody a dustpan for Christmas?" Linda gasped with a laugh in her voice.

I had to smile, too—in part at myself. In almost three weeks, I never even thought about it. Instead, I had scurried around the assembly room of Saukdale Metal Products carrying parts of dustpans for Christmas.

"I can hear somebody opening her Christmas present now," Linda said. "Ooh, a dustpan! It's just what I wanted."

"Oh, you shouldn't have," I laughed in response.

Linda started to giggle. "Why the color matches my broom perfectly! I can't wait to use it. Let's get the kids to track in some dirt."

"Or spill some corn flakes," I added, as tears of laughter began to fill our eyes.

"You know, you have a stupid job, Jim."

We both slowly regained our composure; at least enough so that I could ask about the pet hospital.

"So how was your day?"

"Oh, the usual. We took a couple of dogs out of the running for the Father of the Year award and helped a dumb cat upchuck a ball of its own hair."

"You really don't like cats, do you?"

"I hate cats," Linda answered. "They are mean, calculating, totally selfish animals. A cat will jump on your lap and expect to be petted one minute then turn its back on you and walk away a minute later. They do what they want, when they want, and that's it."

"But you have cats on your farm."

"A farm is the only place cats are of any use, and that's just because they're mean enough to kill mice."

"So," I asked, "if you wanna help sick animals, how can you dislike working on pets so much? Where do you draw the line?"

"I don't dislike it so much. I just see very little value in it. Most pets we treat don't have anything more wrong with them than an uptight owner. So I don't want to spend my life pampering poodles. Okay? I want to help people."

"As a vet?" I kidded playfully.

"Yes, as a veterinarian. I want to help a farmer who can't afford to lose his newborn calves to disease. I want to help a place like Bolivia have healthier herds. That produces more food. Whether you know it or not, there are plenty of countries where poor stock and lack of veterinarians play a direct role in food shortages. Maybe I should bring some professional journals for you to read on the way to Saukdale. I could drive."

If Linda was kidding, her tone didn't sound very playful; and her deep pierc-

35

ing eyes seemed to cut through me as she declared, "It's a big world out there, with big problems. I choose to be involved."

"That'll be pretty hard working with Doc Shelby in West Fork," I offered as a challenge.

"In ten years, probably less," she shot back, "farmers in places like West Fork will be selling breeding stock all over the world. They better have a vet who knows something about the world. Same goes for you dustpan makers. Saukdale Metal Products will be doing international business someday, too. Or, if they aren't careful, some factory in some other country will make a better dustpan and take their place. You wait, the time will come with international trade in just about anything you can imagine."

"Well, I don't think I'll worry just yet about a teacher from another country taking over my seventh- and eighth-grade class."

"No? Then why don't you worry instead about teaching your kids what they'll need to know when they grow up. They better be ready to interact with people from all kinds of countries and cultures."

I didn't know if Linda was right, but I did know that she was way ahead of me. Though I shrugged with feigned indifference, I wondered if those pale blue eyes and sharp black pupils saw through me to my real thoughts. I couldn't tell as she slowly shook her head.

"*Tu eres un tonto*," she muttered in Spanish.

July 4, 1969

Dozens of blankets spread out on the grass formed little cloth islands across the outfield of the softball diamond behind the West Fork Methodist Church. Sawhorses and ropes along the edge of the infield dirt formed a makeshift barrier, and another group of sawhorses supported long planks that stretched diagonally from base line to base line part way between home plate and the pitching rubber. In the rapidly disappearing dusk, anxious children and mothers holding Thermos jugs of Kool-Aid occupied the blankets, while fathers stood nearby talking to their counterparts from the next island over. Everyone awaited the lowering darkness and the beginning of the volunteer firemen's annual Fourth of July fireworks show.

I stood leaning over the new chain-link fence that circled the outfield. I had no one to share a blanket with, and this recent improvement to the softball field beckoned to me as a perfect place to watch the fireworks. It also kept me at a safe distance to avoid a "Hello, Mr. Blair" from every school-age child in the Plum River School District. Though my presence nearby prompted a certain amount of pointing and giggling, I preferred that to an endless string of hellos. In addition, my spot offered a good vantage point from which to see the display of tiny yellow flashes already begun by the lightning bugs in the fence row weeds of the adjacent cornfield.

"Hi, Jim."

The voice from behind caught me by surprise, although I had become more familiar with its sound than any other voice in West Fork.

"Hi, Linda," I said turning quickly. "You told me you didn't like fireworks."

"I don't. I just came to see the people. Will you share your fence with me?"

"That would be nice. Actually, though, I've been watching the lightning bugs more than the people."

"I think I can handle both," she said with a teasing smile.

She's way ahead of me again, I silently teased myself.

With darkness almost completely fallen, Howard Miller, in his position as chief of the one-truck fire department, stepped to the center of the infield to welcome everyone to the fifteenth annual fireworks show. According to Howard, this year's show had five more displays than last year's, including a "spectacular, seven-fountain pyramid."

Howard finished his introduction by inviting the audience to join in the singing of "America the Beautiful." I had learned by now that this was the patriotic song of choice in West Fork. It made a lot of sense. After all, no one could really reach the notes in "The Star-Spangled Banner," and most people shared a bit of uncertainty about the words. Did the bombs bursting in air give proof through the night, or was it through the fight, that our flag was still there? I was never completely confident on that point. In my mind, "America the Beautiful" served as a pretty sensible alternative.

Despite her stated aversion to fireworks, Linda watched the show intently, and I noticed that she gradually slid closer to me, happy, it seemed, to be sharing the display with someone. For twenty-five minutes, rockets shot into the air, pinwheels twirled, cardboard fire engines screamed down the planks, and fountains erupted, all in a hail of brightly colored sparks. The oohs and aahs and the applause left no doubt that this was the biggest night in West Fork since the last Fourth of July. Not a single family stirred from its position when Howard Miller asked for five minutes of patience while the firemen set up the seven-fountain pyramid.

"I heard quite a few 'wows' for a person who doesn't like fireworks."

"It's not the fireworks that I don't like," Linda shot back. "It's what they represent."

"Hey, I was just kidding," I answered, attempting a quick but unsuccessful retreat.

"Maybe you should try being serious once in a while. Then you could think about why we have to use fireworks to represent patriotism. It's just another way to glorify war."

"Come on, fireworks are fun. You have to admit those fountains and pinwheels were pretty."

"And what about the rockets and the bombs? Are loud noises pretty? Why do we call them rockets and bombs? You have kids you teach sitting all over that field. What do they think when a patriotic holiday is all rockets and bombs exploding all over the place? There's a real war right now with real rockets and real bombs and real people dying. You want your kids learning that's the good and patriotic thing to do?"

In that moment, I realized why Linda Bray had chosen to share a piece of the outfield fence with me. She was her father's daughter, taught to speak her mind about what she thought was right. But now, father and daughter had different versions of right, and Don Bray left no doubt about his feelings that supporting our troops and backing the war in Vietnam was right. If this had been a chicken barbecue instead of a show of patriotism, the father and his equally outspoken daughter might have sat side by side. For the Fourth of July fireworks, Linda stood at the fence; and for the moment she stood staring hard at me, waiting for an answer, any answer, to her barrage of questions.

"Okay," I said, "I just don't think you have to make a cause or a crusade out of everything."

"Look, without standing up for causes, nothing will ever change. To me, a person has to try to make things better. So call that a crusade if you want. I'm going to crusade if it helps things. I guess you just want to stand aside all the time. What do you think a person should do?"

Linda and I stood face to face. Words would not come to me.

"Well, I just try..." I began haltingly, "I try to live my own life to...to treat ...to treat people fair in what I do. I think that's a way to make the world better."

Behind me the lighting of the seven fountains interrupted my stammering speech. In the glow created by the yellow, green, red, and white sparks, I could see moisture welling up in Linda's eyes.

"If everybody was like you, Jim," she said gently, "the world would be a better place. Hey, look, you're missing the pyramid."

In Linda's glistening eyes, I could see the reflection of sparks from the large, red center fountain.

"Beautiful," I whispered to myself before slowly turning my own eyes back to the field.

July 24, 1969

Dreary gray clouds blanketed the late afternoon sky as I walked across the Saukdale Metal Products parking lot. A few scattered drops continued to splash into the puddles left by the steady, monotonous rain that had fallen most of the day. The break in the showers allowed me to reach my car with only a few drops of water spotting my dark blue work shirt, but the drenching of everything in sight that already had occurred left no doubt that my plans to watch tonight's softball game at the Methodist Church diamond had been washed away by the weather. Right now, I didn't care. The workday was over, and I looked forward to my ride home with Linda.

The half-hour drives between West Fork and Saukdale had become my favorite parts of the day. While I drove, Linda assumed a comfortable pose, turned toward me with one leg tucked up under her on the seat. She would lay her left arm on the seat back with her hand extending toward me and inching closer with each change of subject in our conversation. Our talk followed pathways as twisting and turning as the road from West Fork to Saukdale was straight and true. Even if her fingertips never quite touched my shoulder in the space of the twenty-five-mile trip, our conversations seemed to touch every imaginable topic. How to wash a car. (I said soap the windows first, she said just start at the top.) Why people eat liver. (A mystery to us both.) Living in New York City. (A subject long on opinions, though neither of us had ever been there.) Her aversion to cats. (Powerful, to say the least.) The best television shows. (We actually agreed on *My World and Welcome to It*.) The war. (A subject impossible to avoid.) Herman's Hermits. (An inexplicable interest.) Pepsi versus Coke. (We didn't agree.) Pre-marital sex. (It was an individual decision, we nobly decided.) The best place to watch a sunset. (I said over the Mississippi River. She said I was too provincial.) Every day the talk and the miles flew by.

Linda stood waiting outside the front door as I came to a stop at Griffin's Pet Hospital. The lingering light rain from the drab, gray sky suggested a position inside the glass double doors as the better place to stand, but I knew Linda. Linda did as Linda saw fit and rarely bowed to concerns so conventional as the weather. Today, she waited outside in the light rain. Tomorrow, I might have to seek her out in Dr. Griffin's waiting room, lost in the pages of some professional journal and oblivious to time.

"Hi," I said as she slid onto the front seat and closed the door behind her.

She sat facing forward and gave a slight shiver as the rain outside began to pick up again.

"Looks like we might be in for rain all night," I said.

"Yeah."

"Have a tough day?" I asked, as much in response to her straight ahead posture as to her one-syllable answer to my hello.

"It was okay."

Her words said okay but her tone said don't ask. I turned onto the highway and headed toward West Fork.

"Don't feel good?" I let another innocent question slip out.

"I'm okay," came the quick, terse answer.

I sat quietly for a moment, resolved to refrain from asking even the simplest question.

The rhythmic sound of the windshield wipers in the steady rain played a monotonous accompaniment to the familiar sights of the landscape rolling by along the highway. If the sights and sounds along the route from West Fork to Saukdale typically offered little to remark upon, the smells were an entirely different matter. On many a drive, the odors from a nearby barnyard would overwhelm all the other senses. Freshly spread manure or a breeze blowing through a farrowing house would temporarily fill the car with the unmistakable scents of livestock farming. Most farmers called it the smell of money.

We had barely passed the city limits when the smells began to build up in the old green Falcon. Unlike other days, this odor hung in the damp air with unusual persistence. Whatever the source of the potent smell, it could not be the product of any single farm. In that case, we would have driven away from it. Yet, rather than dissipating, the odor seemed to grow stronger with each passing mile.

"What is that smell?" I said finally, breaking my self-imposed embargo on questions.

"Huh?"

"That smell," I repeated. "It just keeps getting stronger."

"Look, I know," Linda snapped.

"But do you know what it is?" I pressed.

"It's me." Her face flushed red.

"What is it?" Another question popped out.

"A cat."

"What kind of cat smells like that?"

"A plain old stupid cat. Okay? We had to give a cat shots today and it got away. When I grabbed it, it soiled my foot."

"Soiled your foot?"

"It pissed on my foot!" Her voice rose in anger. "I caught the damn cat and it pissed on my foot. Is that what you want to hear? It pissed on my foot. I don't know why it pissed on my foot. It just pissed on my foot!"

"Maybe it knows how you feel about cats," I laughed without thinking.

Linda did not laugh. Instead, her cheeks blazed and her deep black pupils shot a look straight through me.

"In that case," she answered with a tremor in her words, "I better keep my feet away from you."

I couldn't tell whether the quiver in her voice marked anger, embarrassment, or both. I could tell that the problem with her foot was not nearly so severe as the problem with the foot I had stuck in my mouth. No trip to West Fork ever seemed longer as the interminable minutes hung in the air like the acrid odor coming from the passenger side of the car.

August 28, 1969

Linda suggested the picnic, and Linda chose the place. Both caught me by surprise. Yesterday, she finished her summer job at the pet hospital, and we took our last ride together to Saukdale. By next week, she would be back in class at Michigan A&E. Some kind of goodbye did seem appropriate. Still, her suggestion of a picnic at the old Lone Oak School surprised me.

As we turned into the drive, I realized that a year to the day had passed since I pulled up in front of this old building to meet Miss Fredericks and save a school bell. Nature had weathered the empty building only a little in that time. Yet, somehow, the old school now seemed much more like a relic.

"This is where I went to school. Not very big, is it?" Linda reached for the grocery bag on the seat between us.

She had shopped for the picnic yesterday, and the contents of the bag remained a carefully guarded secret. Little secrets and surprises appeared to be the order of the day in her plans.

"Would you grab the blanket from the back, Jim? I know a really neat place down the hill."

I followed her behind the building and down the long grade toward the east fork of the Plum River. The sloping hillside added an extra spring to Linda's always bounding stride.

"You can't see it from here, but there's a little island in the bend of the river," she said. "It's over the fence from school property and hidden by trees on both banks. It's actually on the back corner of our farm. Miss Fredericks never let us kids go over the fence or near the river. I don't think anyone even knows the island's there."

Her words spilled out faster with each step, and I could barely keep up with either the talk or the walk by the time we reached the bottom of the hill. We slipped through some tall weeds then threaded our way between the gnarled trunks of a tightly planted hedge row.

Linda pointed to a rusty barbed wire fence. "Dad used to pasture this end of the farm, but he has it in a government set aside now. Spread the fence, and I'll go through first."

I put one foot on the middle wire and pulled up on the top strand. Linda ducked through with the casual assurance gathered in growing up on a farm. As she parted the wires for me, I took my turn more gingerly but eased past the barbs without snagging my shirt or pants.

Safely through the fence, we stood at the edge of the east fork of the Plum River. At this point, the river amounted to nothing more than a small creek bending between two low hills. In the floor of this tiny valley, the creek divided around a gravelly patch of land to form a little island with a small thatch of green grass in the center.

"Take 'em off," she said, rolling up her pants legs and unlacing her shoes.

I followed her orders and waded barefoot into the shallow waters, which felt much cooler than I expected. I was sure she chuckled to herself as I feigned nonchalance at the chill of the water. She probably laughed at my feet, too. I had never noticed how ugly they were. Now a surge of embarrassment and urgency to cover those feet welled up inside me.

With the stream safely forded, I paused to slip on my shoes, but Linda grabbed me by the arm. "Come here, Jim. Lay the blanket on the grass."

She tossed her shoes to the side with enough flourish to leave no doubt that she expected me to do the same. The feet would have to show, even the crooked pinky that always hid in my left shoe. Linda took a spot on the blanket with her feet and legs curled up neatly underneath her. As the thirty or so square yards of island held little potential for exploration, I stretched out on the blanket as well, my less-than-limber legs unable to fold up into the neat package that Linda presented.

"I've loved this place ever since I was little. It's almost like my own hidden world," she sighed.

"That's neat," I said, not wanting to reveal that her grade school teacher had told me about this place on my second day in West Fork.

"Okay, did you have a special place when you were a kid?"

"Not really . . . I guess sometimes at night I pretended my bed could fly."

"Uh-huh, so how is that like having your own island?"

"Well, I just pretended I could fly in my bed anywhere, over anything in the world. No matter where I went or what was going on, nobody could get me on my flying bed. It was safe no matter what."

"Some fantasy. Did your parents try to get you help?"

"Hey, look, I was real young. Okay?"

"I'm just kidding. It's actually kind of cute," she said.

"I think an island is probably better. I mean, you still have the island."

"So your bed doesn't fly anymore?"

"If it did, I'd keep it a secret."

"But I'm good at finding out secrets."

"I'm afraid that's a talent you're wasting on me. I don't have any good secrets."

"But you do have things you don't talk about very much."

"Like?" I asked.

"Like teaching school. You start back next week and you haven't even mentioned it. Is it nice getting out of the factory, you know, getting back to teaching?"

Maybe I did keep secrets. I knew I didn't want to tell Linda the truth. Actually, that wasn't quite it, either. I was too embarrassed, too afraid, too shy, too something, to tell Linda the truth. I didn't want school to start. By the time school started, Linda would be back in Michigan. I had thought very little about the start of school. Instead, the end of summer filled my thoughts. The end of summer meant the end of seeing Linda five days a week, the end of seeing her until who knew when. But how could I tell her the truth? I hadn't even mustered up the courage to ask her for a date all summer. Even this picnic was her idea. How could the same person who never made the slightest move toward asking her out now tell Linda Bray how much he would miss her?

"See. There you go, or there you don't go. You won't even talk to me about being a teacher. I'd really like to know how you feel. If you dislike teaching too much to talk about it, I wonder why you do it."

"I can tell you things if it's really important to you," I answered without telling her anything at all.

"I just said it's important."

"Why?"

"Because teaching is important. Because I think kids need good teachers. Because I like kids. Because I like you. Because of everything. Because of my dad. Because, because, because."

I wondered if anybody could talk faster than Linda when she was excited. I also wondered if she liked me the way she liked kids or if she liked me differently. But I asked the question that I wondered about the most, "What do you mean, because of your dad?"

"You know how he feels about things. I've told you."

Linda said "things" and I knew what she meant. Between Linda and her father, "things" meant only one thing, the war in Vietnam.

"You have another argument about the war?"

"Not really. If we talk about it at all, it's just some version of the same old argument. You know."

I did know. And I also knew that I skirted talking about the war anytime I could. Now, somehow, Linda wanted to talk to me about teaching school because she had argued with her dad about Vietnam.

"Dad just starts on everything," she said. "He says we could win the war in six months if people in this country would face up to it and do it. As far as he's concerned, that's how we won World War II, and Vietnam's a lot smaller. You can't talk about what's right or wrong. If somebody doesn't agree with him, that person's a traitor or a draft-dodger or just stupid."

"And men with teaching deferments are draft-dodgers?" I asked.

"He didn't say anything about you, Jim. But I . . . you don't ever bring up why . . . what you like about teaching."

"So maybe I am a draft-dodger?"

The emotion rose in my voice. I hoped Linda heard anger. If she heard anger, and not fear, maybe she wouldn't push the question, the question I was afraid to ask myself.

"Jim, that's not what I said."

"Well then, what does the war have to do with teaching?"

"Nothing. Nothing. That's just it, nothing, and I'm so tired of everything between Dad and me turning back to the war. I'm not going to change the way I am. If something is wrong, you speak up."

Ironically, at the words *speak up* we both fell into an awkward silence. I looked over at the stream, unwilling to ask myself, much less answer to another, how I truly felt about the war. Linda slowly twirled the grass at the edge of the blanket between her fingers, unwilling perhaps, to let this responsibility to speak up invade her private little island any further.

A minute passed like five in the strained silence, until my suddenly churning stomach offered a clearly audible growl. We looked at each other, and two slightly foolish smiles began to creep ever so gently across our faces.

"Hungry?" she asked.

"I guess so," I replied, thankful for the first time in my life for the intrusion of a bodily noise into a social situation.

Linda flashed her own smile of relief and amusement. She reached over for the grocery bag in which she had packed our picnic.

"I hope you like what I brought," she said with some of her earlier buoyancy returning to her voice.

After producing paper cups and plates and napkins, she pulled a large, covered plastic bowl from the bag. A bakery loaf of rye bread, a jar of brown mustard, and two smaller, square plastic containers next joined the array on the blanket.

"I've got a bottle of wine, too," she said.

While the big plastic bowl seemed a perfect size for fried chicken, the two small containers, the rye bread, and the jar of mustard hinted at ham and cheese sandwiches. Maybe the bowl held potato salad.

"Here, Jim, slice some bread."

She handed me a knife as she opened the big bowl to reveal a large bunch of grapes, two apples, and a pear. A chunk of Cheddar cheese and one of Muenster appeared from the smaller containers. She placed slices of apple and pear on my plate and reached for the bread I had cut.

"Try this mustard on the bread with some cheese," she said. "It's really good."

After her flurry of arranging, opening, and slicing, Linda finally glanced my way once again. Her eyes read the poorly disguised befuddlement of a small-town guy and his twenty-three years of experience with fried chicken, potato salad, and baked beans as picnic fare.

"*Sorprendido?*" came her comment in Spanish.

I never knew what Linda said in Spanish, but I always knew how she meant it. It should have made me mad. It would have made me mad. Except, it always caught me off guard. I took a bite of the Cheddar on rye with mustard. The brown mustard tingled on my tongue and made the next bite of the freshly sliced apple taste even sweeter. Inside, I smiled. Linda was way ahead of me again.

"Good?" she asked.

"Real good," I nodded.

"I have friends in the music department at Laurel College. In the spring, this is what we always take on picnics."

Linda handed me a paper cup of rosé wine.

"To our summer," she toasted.

I lifted my cup to her toast, caught off guard again. Our summer? It sounded good, whatever it meant. I wanted to ask, but a different question came to my lips.

"So, do you spend a lot of time at this Laurel College?"

"It's not very far from the A&E campus; and in a roundabout way, Laurel is the reason I went to A&E. It's funny to talk about it here. Miss Fredericks, my teacher up the hill, went to Laurel. The very first time I told her I wanted to be a veterinarian, she talked to me about Michigan A&E. I must have been about nine or ten years old."

Linda turned her head toward the school hill across the stream then looked back at me.

"Anyway, when I ended up there, she said I should go over to Laurel for some of their plays and concerts. For a small college, their theater and music really has a great reputation. I enjoyed things—the performances—and pretty soon, you know, you just make friends."

From the light in her eyes as she spoke, they must have been important friends. Yet, she had never talked to me about any of them. This between two people who had managed, over the course of the summer, to discuss everything from Herman's Hermits to their favorite Christmas presents as children.

"You never mentioned having friends at another college. I guess I figured you hung out mostly with vet school people."

"I like lots of different kinds of people," she said. "I don't always mix them together. Maybe I see different worlds with different people."

"I suppose that makes sense, but we've talked about so many things. I'm kinda curious, hearing about something all new like this."

"Well, curiosity killed the cat," she teased.

"So what," I said. "You hate cats."

"That's right," she snapped.

The bite in Linda's voice said back off, but the softness in her eyes said something else.

"Here, hold still, Jim."

She leaned toward me and gently touched her napkin to my cheek.

"You don't have to save that mustard," she said with a grin. "We have plenty left."

As I smiled and glanced toward the ground, the napkin dropped from Linda's hand. Her fingers slid across my cheek and behind my neck, lightly brushing the back of my hair. In a single motion, she drew me toward her and pressed her lips against mine in a long, firm kiss.

"I've wanted to do that for a long time," she whispered.

"Me, too."

"Well then, it's okay to kiss back," she said, lying down on the blanket.

I eased back next to her. My left arm curled under her as she drew closer to me. Our lips met again. Lying in a halo of sunlight framed by the trees, we held the kiss until all sense of time and place seemed to disappear. I brushed my fingers lightly against her hair, feeling like I needed to touch her with more than my kiss just to be sure this moment was real. Almost imperceptibly, she parted her lips and ran the tip of her tongue along my mouth. I followed her lead, slowly and gently exploring with my tongue.

"Mm, that's nice," she said in a low, private voice.

"I know." I searched for words as my body filled with sensation. "You really . . ."

"Shh, listen. Hear how quiet it is?" Linda nuzzled against my cheek and reached down to unbutton her blouse.

She watched as I opened my shirt, too. Her small breasts lay flat, but I felt foolish as I remembered our first drive to Saukdale and my pouting thoughts about her flat chest. Now, she seemed so delicate, almost like a piece of porcelain too fine to touch.

Linda drew my hand to her chest as we kissed again. Her fingers ran across my skin with a soft, sensuous touch like nothing I had ever felt before. A light tingle rose at each place she touched until even the slightest movement of her hand made a stronger, more intense excitement flow through me.

I tried to return the exquisite sensation to her with my fingertips moving in slow circles barely touching her skin. While we kissed, I felt her chest rise and fall as each breath came warmer and deeper. I lightly ran each of my fingertips across her firm nipples, making them grow even harder.

With her fingers exploring my chest and stomach, her caress and mine seemed to become one as I lowered the soft, circular movement of my fingertips down to her stomach. Linda gave a quick jerk and a small gasp.

"Ticklish?" I asked gently. She only kissed me harder.

Time meant nothing as we kissed and touched. Our fingers continued to move slowly, searching for new spots to fill with sensation. Gradually, each motion took me lower and lower on her stomach. I loosened the top button on her jeans. My fingers felt her silky underwear then ran along the length of her waist where the panties met her skin. I began to move my touch under the elastic and felt her jerk again, stronger and harder than last time.

She took my hand in hers and put her lips to my ear.

"Not today, Jim."

Her words came in a voice gentler and more intimate than any I had ever heard.

"I just wanted you to . . ." I started.

"I already did," she whispered in the same voice. "Twice."

Deep inside me, all the sensation of her touch merged with some new emotion—partly a smile for Linda, partly a tear for the closeness, partly a laugh at myself. Maybe Linda Bray would always be way ahead of me.

October 28, 1969

Cold gray skies and a harsh wind off the western Illinois prairie caught me more than slightly by surprise and totally dismayed the students of the Plum River Elementary School seventh and eighth grades. The day's predicted high of forty-one fell almost twenty degrees short of the normal temperatures for the last week in October.

Weather hadn't crossed my mind two weeks ago when I planned this experiment to conclude our math unit. Of course, my kids hadn't planned, or possibly even thought at all, when they grabbed their light jackets as they headed for school this morning. I was probably just lucky that they all had coats, even if none were warm enough for current conditions. Now, we stood shivering together on the softball diamond behind the West Fork Methodist Church.

"Mr. Blair, do we have to do this?" Jane Marshal whined.

"Well, you kids said there's nothing useful about the math we've been studying. I'm going to show you how triangulation can be used to measure distances."

"But it's *freezing.*"

"*I'm* freezing."

"I'm *frozen.*"

The voices came faster than I could count and louder than I liked.

"All right, settle down. If you pay some attention, this will be fun. We're going to triangulate the distance down the rightfield line."

"I think it would be more fun to triangulate the distance across the gym where it's warm," Jane Marshal said with a note very near to disgust in her voice.

Jane led the way in academic performance among my nine eighth-grade students. She seemed always to have the right answer, the right action, and the right attitude for every situation—at least until today. My two grades totaled sixteen students, and during the first two months of school, only five had avoided being banished from class to the hall for some infraction. Among those five, only Jane had not come close—at least until today.

While Jane and the other girls complained, the boys adopted the more practical strategy of huddling against the shelter of a small shed located a few yards behind the backstop. From this vantage point, they could make out virtually nothing of the valuable lesson in triangulation I attempted to demonstrate for them.

"Come on guys," I yelled. "You can't help from over there."

The young mathematicians grudgingly gathered around home plate with me, although the only number they cared about at the moment was the one that measured degrees Fahrenheit.

"If we put a stake here and another one part way down the third base line," I said, "we can form a triangle with the point down where the rightfield line meets the fence."

I kneeled down to drive the first stake into the ground as my students crowded close together against the cold. A faint chorus of giggles greeted my efforts when several good hammer blows to the stake produced only a loose purchase in the hard-packed dirt of the softball diamond.

"First, we can measure the short leg of the triangle on the third base line," I continued. "Next, we know that the two base lines form a right angle, and finally, we mark the other angle in the dirt from our point down the third base line by sighting to the fence where it meets the rightfield line. That gives us what we need."

By now, I realized what we all really needed were warm hats and gloves. I poured out my complicated lesson faster and faster as the biting wind accelerated.

"Simple subtraction will let us find the third angle. That gives us one leg of the triangle and all three angles. We can calculate the length of the rightfield line to the fence without measuring it. Everybody understand?"

Sixteen shivering kids with glazed eyes nodded yes. Today's great experiment obviously left my students cold, figuratively and literally.

"It still won't work if we're all too frozen to move," Jane said.

"Well then, you can walk the measuring tape down the third base line," I told her. "That way you'll be moving."

"I don't see why we can't just measure the rightfield line if we want to know," Jane answered back.

"We will," I explained, "when we're done, to check our results."

"Well, if we're going to measure anyway . . ."

"Jane, that's enough," I barked. "You're out of this class."

Temporarily removing disruptive kids from class had served as my standard form of discipline, and I felt it had worked well—most of the time. Now, I realized I had effectively kicked Jane Marshal off of the cold softball diamond and into a warm hallway at the school. The spring in her step betrayed the feigned look of hurt on her face as Jane obediently, and quickly, headed back toward the school. Maybe the members of the female population of West Fork learned the art of staying one step ahead of the men at an early age.

"All right, the rest of you come with me, and we'll put in the second flag."

As I kneeled down working the stake into the ground, I heard the voice of Jane's best friend, Diane Sandstrom, behind me.

"Mr. Blair, Timmy Stevens' dog just stole the other flag."

I wheeled around from my kneeling position to see a long-haired, brown mutt romping out toward centerfield with one of my two stakes in its mouth. The quiet, frozen faces of fifteen children suddenly broke into giggles, and almost as quickly, half of the group gave chase.

While my students pursued Fido or Spot or Rex to no avail, I realized that my carefully designed experiment did not include a backup stake in the event of encountering a flag-pilfering pet. As the little dog bolted around the outfield fence and headed toward the cemetery, I also realized that the possibility of regaining my composure, much less control of the class, roughly matched the likelihood of retrieving the flag.

"Class. Class! *Class*!!" My voice rose in three successive steps to the loudest shout I could muster.

With the force of the last scream, the kids running around the outfield downshifted from a gallop to a trot, then to an aimless walk followed finally by a few tentative steps back in my direction. Those who had not joined in the chase took their own small steps backward in response to the unexpected explosion of my voice.

53

Eventually, all eyes turned to me. In those eyes, I read a measure of surprise and a whisper of fear. I didn't mind the surprise. I felt embarrassed by the fear.

"All right, everybody back to the school. If you can't control yourselves when we try something special, then we'll just go back to the textbook. When we get inside, I want all of you to take out your math books and do all five enrichment problems at the bottom of page forty-six."

Enrichment problems. I doubted that they had ever enriched anyone. Half of the time, I didn't understand how to do them myself or how they related to the lessons they accompanied. I suspected that they represented the textbook writers' eccentric, pet ideas, rescued from the editor's wastebasket and given the name *enrichment problems*. Today, however, the downtrodden looks that passed over the faces of my students proved that the enrichment problems had served their purpose. Today, they were punishment problems.

Some mistakes had to be punished to maintain discipline; and in a long tradition of education, everyone had to pay the price for the mistakes of a few people, or in this case, one person: me. Unfortunately, like an umpire caught in a bad call, I couldn't change my decision now. The kids would have to do the enrichment problems. I would spend my time thinking about where I could find some extra special Halloween treats for the seventh and eighth graders of the Plum River Elementary School.

November 27, 1969

"Jim, would you wash my back?"

The coy urging in Linda's voice roused me from the deep peace that enveloped me as I lay listening to the muffled sound of the shower running in the bath of our room at the Northport City Center Motel. Whether or not Northport, Wisconsin's population of twenty-six thousand people constituted a city might be an open question in some minds, but at least the motel lived up to the second half of its name. The building stood on a corner only one block from Northport's harbor and absolutely in the center of downtown. And even if it wasn't the epitome of big city luxury, the new carpet, ribbed bedspread and abstract prints, all in shades of tangerine, made me appreciate what my teacher's salary could afford for a room. It surely beat where Linda and I might have stayed if both of us were still students.

"Be right there," I answered, eager for any reason to feel Linda close to me.

Five quick steps took me into the bathroom and proved the practicality of sleeping in the nude. With no clothes to cast off, I simply pulled back the shower curtain and stepped into the tub. Linda stood with her back toward me as the warm water cascaded from the shower head down over her face and body.

"Here," she said, handing a bar of soap backwards over her shoulder.

I gently rubbed the soap into a foamy white lather on her back. I thrilled at the touch of her soft, pale skin yet wondered at the same time just who this woman was. As I ran my hands over her narrow shoulders, small frame, slender arms, and smooth, unblemished skin, Linda seemed almost fragile; but moving down her back, Linda's body tapered into round, firm hips with strong, well-muscled legs. It was as if her body formed a physical expression of the contradictions in her personality—sometimes gentle and quiet, sometimes sharp and assertive. Her gentle side broke into my thoughts as she handed me a washcloth thoroughly soaked in warm water.

"Here, use this," she said.

I took the washcloth from her hand, slowly wiping the soap away down the length of her back and over her behind.

"Mm, that feels good," she sighed.

I wrapped my arms around her from behind and held Linda close. I felt the warmth of her body touch my skin, then flow deep within my chest. In some indescribable mixture of emotion and excitement, I felt myself grow hard as the curve of her hips rubbed against me.

"Don't you ever stop?" she giggled. "I think that last night and this morning should have been enough for you. Besides, I have a boat to catch."

She slipped out of my arms and stepped deftly from the tub.

"Maybe you need a cold shower," she teased, quickly turning off the hot water knob.

I shook from the sudden icy stream of cold water. Linda shook in laughter.

"You're gonna get it!" I shouted and climbed out of the tub with the water still running.

She dashed out the bathroom door with her towel trailing behind and me close at her heels.

"Nowhere to go," I laughed.

I grabbed Linda around the waist and pulled her onto the unmade bed. I reached for the towel and tousled her short hair into a tangled mess as we rolled over the covers. We came to rest with Linda on top of me, her ruffled hair standing on end. I pulled her close to me for a kiss, but we both began to laugh too hard to bring our lips together. She lay with her face buried against my neck as we quaked with laughter. Finally, she raised her lips to my ear.

"I love you," she whispered.

"I love you, too."

"I wish we could stay like this forever," she said in a voice we both knew meant the time to part was near.

We lay embracing silently for a few seconds then Linda gently edged over to the side of the bed and sighed as she reached for her watch on the nightstand. I broke the silence for her.

"Let me shave while you get dressed. I know it's getting late."

I wished, as Linda did, for a way to make time stand still, but the mundane acts of shaving, pulling on clothes, and shoving my things into a bag seemed to propel time forward. Within twenty minutes, we were seated in the motel coffee shop. Less than an hour remained until the Northport car ferry would leave for Michigan. Directed by the demands of time, we both ordered only toast and coffee. I sipped my coffee and raised again the subject we had discussed yesterday.

"I still don't see why I can't drive you to Laurel," I said.

"I just like the ferry," she answered.

"I know, but we could spend more time together if I drove you. Don't you like me more than the ferry?"

"Okay, I'll tell you the truth. I like you, but I don't like your car. I don't want to drive all the way to Michigan in a car with no radio."

"Come on, I'm serious."

"And I'm serious about riding the ferry." A different tone entered her voice. "People use cars all the time—like there's no other way to travel. And you know what? If they keep it up long enough, there won't be any other way. No trains, no busses, no ferries, no nothing."

"But you told me this ferry basically carries railroad cars across the lake. How much difference does it make if you ride?"

"Who knows, but I'm going to make all the difference I can. You can argue all you want. I'm going to ride the ferry as long as there's one to ride."

"Look, I'm not arguing. It's just the time together I'm talking about."

"No, you're arguing. People must think that I came for Thanksgiving just to argue. If everybody already knows how I feel about things, why do we even have to talk about it?"

Just that suddenly, we weren't talking about the ferry. We weren't talking about me. We were talking about Linda and her father. I knew the tension between them increased every time she came home. Now, I also knew why she had said so little about Thanksgiving on the drive to Northport.

"I understand what you're saying," I said. "Let's get you down to the ferry. I really want to see the boat."

"Ship, Jim. It's big. They call it a ship."

"Does that mean I have to say *bon voyage*?" I kidded as we headed out the coffee shop door.

"No, it means you have to hold me very tight and kiss me."

I did.

February 16, 1970

Cold air bit at my bare fingers as I stepped out of the little post office in the side room of Hazel Anderson's house. The cold meant little to me. I had to open the letter—the letter from Linda.

February 13, 1970

Dear Jim,

    I hated to hang up tonight. As soon as I did, I grabbed this piece of paper. I can still hear the sound of your voice, and I just want it to last a little longer.

    I'm glad you think the boys are doing better at basketball. I bet you'll win some games this year. If you don't get discouraged, the kids won't either.

    It's snowing pretty hard outside. I forgot to tell you that. It seems like we have so little time to talk when you call that I forget to tell you or ask you lots of things. Is it snowing in West Fork? Sometimes I wonder about funny things or maybe think about things at funny times. You know most of our time together in West Fork has been summer. I wonder what you look like walking down the street with snow all around.

I'd like to see you just shoveling your sidewalk or maybe build a snowman with you.

Jim, I love it when you call, but I hate it when it's over. I can't wait until we're together. Spring break seems so far away.

You can probably tell by now that I really don't have anything important to say. I should close. I just didn't want our time to be over.

I love you.

Linda

Linda's words warmed me through, but I must have been a sight slowly strolling toward the West Fork Store with my nose buried in a letter as if the cold February morning was a balmy summer day. Fortunately for my public image, not a single car passed by and nobody seemed to be stirring. In a place as small as West Fork, that could happen. Of course, people talked about everything they saw, but some days there was just nothing there to see, and other days there was just nobody there to see it. I stuffed Linda's letter into my shirt pocket and opened the door to the West Fork Store.

"Morning, Jim," came the greeting from two regulars in the Saturday donut club.

"Hi, Doc. Hi, Howard," I responded with a wave.

"You'll have to get your own donut and coffee today, Jim," I heard Margaret Dublin's voice call from the back. "We're right in the middle of a project."

I turned and saw Bill Dublin perched on a stepladder with Margaret handing him a screwdriver.

"What's going on?" I asked.

"I'm helping Bill put up new window shades."

"Yeah, if I start to fall, she's going to yell 'Look out!'" Bill said with a grin.

"Never mind about the smart remarks," Margaret said. "Just put up that bracket before you do fall."

I filled a coffee cup, grabbed my usual chocolate donut, and marveled at Bill and Margaret. If ever anything should be the cause of marital discord, surely putting together roller shades might top the list. Yet, there were Bill and Margaret, yards of material and every tool in the place spread out in front of them, still looking like the happiest couple in the world. Maybe they were.

"It must be nice to really belong in a place," I said to Howard and Doc as I settled into a chair.

"How so?" Doc asked.

"Well, look at Margaret and Bill. They own the store here. They must have known each other all of their lives. It seems like they're exactly where they belong."

"They might belong here, Jim," Doc said, "but they sure haven't known each other all their lives."

"I'd say about twenty-five or twenty-six years," Howard added.

"But, if they grew up in West Fork . . ." I started.

"Oh, no," said Doc, "they met during the war. Neither one of them is from West Fork. Bill's from someplace in Iowa. Margaret, she's from Wisconsin. Bill was in the Navy, stationed at the Great Lakes training base. That's not too far from where Margaret lived. How long have they had the store, Howard?"

"Must be about twenty-three years," Howard answered. "I enlisted in the Army at eighteen. I got out in 1946, and Bill and Margaret bought the store about eight months after I got home. Spring of '47. I remember because old Bill Johnston had the store for probably thirty years before that. I thought it was kind of a coincidence—two guys named Bill owning the store right in a row. There's a hundred names that could have been, but we've had two guys named Bill for more than fifty years."

"Yeah, 1947 sounds about right to me," Doc said.

Howard unconsciously rubbed two fingers against his chin as he yelled to Bill, "Say, Bill, when did you and Margaret buy the store?"

"1947. Must have been about March."

"No, May," Margaret corrected.

"Just like I thought," Howard nodded to Doc and me. "I got out of the Army in '46. It was the nineteenth of September. They bought the store eight months later."

"Why'd you want to know?" Bill called over from his ladder.

"Oh, Jim here thought you and Margaret probably grew up in West Fork."

"No," Bill laughed. "We got here by accident. Margaret had an aunt who lived a couple hours south of here. We were just driving through when we saw the for sale sign on the store. I was working in a mattress factory and just decided I'd rather work for myself."

"Then how come out of the two of you, Margaret's the one that works here ten hours a day?" Howard joked to Bill.

In addition to the store, Bill drove one of the two Plum River Elementary School busses, and he clerked for the Spenceville Auction Service. Margaret, you always found at the store.

"I figured out that having Margaret do the work was even better than working for myself," Bill answered with his big grin growing even wider.

"Well, right now, you can work on this shade, or I might be the one to dump you off this ladder," Margaret said.

"Those old shades have been there thirty years," Howard said to Margaret. "Ten more minutes shouldn't hurt anything."

"You're no help, Howard Miller," Margaret scolded. "Drink your coffee and talk to those other two yardbirds."

The opening of the store's front door added a punctuation mark to Margaret's command.

"Morning, Don," Howard said, looking up at the new arrival.

Don Bray was not a regular at Saturday morning coffee, but he enjoyed a status in West Fork that always evoked extra, even solicitous, attention. Small places don't forget their heroes, from sports or from war. Don Bray, decorated Navy man and the area's best shortstop ever, was both.

"What do you need, Don?" Bill Dublin asked as he started down from his ladder.

"I'm cutting out a dead elm at the southeast corner of my place, out by the road. It's not very big, but I don't want it dropping limbs on a fence. Anyway, I'm out of bar oil for my chainsaw. You know how that elm will dull a saw. I thought if you had some plain 10-weight motor oil, I could use that. I don't want to run over to the hardware in Spenceville just for some bar oil."

"I've got some in the back," said Bill. "Most people want 10 W 30 nowadays, but I always keep a couple of cans of ten-weight on hand."

"Here, Don," Doc Shelby piped in, "why don't you sit down and have a cup of coffee. I've been watching Bill try to put up one window shade the whole time I've been here. If he gets all the way off that ladder, Margaret will never have new shades in this place."

"Well, maybe a quick cup," Don said.

"You take it black, don't you?" Margaret asked, pouring a cup. Of course, she already knew the answer to her question, just as she knew to reach a powdered donut from the box on the counter.

"Thanks, Margaret," Don said. "It's a pretty cold one this morning. A hot cup of coffee might just warm me up a little."

"My thermometer read ten degrees this morning at seven," Howard said. "This is the coldest winter in at least twenty years. We've had nine nights below zero so far. I'll bet two or three more would be a record."

"Well, we shouldn't have any more," Don stated.

"That's true," Doc agreed. "It's getting pretty late in the season for below zero weather."

Don Bray turned toward me and turned the conversation to even warmer days to come.

"Linda says you're picking her up for spring break."

"Yeah, I'm driving up to Northport to meet the ferry."

"I don't understand that for the life of me," Don said. "You drive all the way up to Wisconsin when it would be faster for her just to come straight home. The train comes right to Saukdale."

"Linda says she wants to support the ferry because of its history. You know, to help keep it in business."

"The last time I looked trains were historic, too. They could use some business of their own. I don't think one girl riding partway to school is going to keep boats operating on the Great Lakes."

"You know Linda," I offered weakly, hoping to escape the conversation.

"I know her. I've known her twenty-two years longer than you have," Don answered without a smile.

"I don't care how she gets here," Doc interjected. "You two just be sure to tell her to come talk to me when she's home. I want her back for the summer. She's the best help I ever had. I missed her last year."

"Serves you right for making her work for that pet doctor." Don's face brightened as he turned toward Doc. "I think she hated every minute of last summer."

I thought back to that time and knew that Linda had not hated every minute of the summer. So many minutes were our time together. Besides, I had seen her change and even acknowledge that she might have done some good helping people with their sick pets. Linda never hated doing good. I wondered why Don Bray hadn't seen the change in his daughter. Maybe it was just being a parent.

As a teacher, I was starting to see parents and children through new eyes. How often do parents really see their children change? Even their grown children. Do they notice the small, almost imperceptible, steps through which people mature, or do parents wake up with rude jolts at points in their children's lives and wonder where these different people came from? It seemed to me that Linda Bray came to her father in jolts.

Whatever the truth in these thoughts, they were ones to keep carefully concealed, just as I hoped my shirt pocket adequately concealed Linda's distinctive handwriting on the envelope I received in the morning mail. Doc Shelby already had saved me from an awkward conversation. Now, Bill Dublin completed the rescue by appearing from the back of the store with a can of ten-weight oil. As everyone's attention returned to the operation of chainsaws, I quietly excused myself and headed out into the cold February morning.

March 30, 1970

Spring would be late this year. Matted brown weeds lay in the fence rows and filled the ditches along the gravel road to the Bray farm. So far, none of the usual soaking rains or occasional warm days that tempted you to pop outside in your shirtsleeves had visited the rolling prairies of western Illinois. The grass in the farmyards carried only a faint green tint and buds poked out very tentatively on the tree limbs. Both awaited a clearer sign that the land would renew its cycle of life.

The dirty brown landscape and overcast gray sky matched my mood. Linda's week of spring break had been all too short. For some reason, I couldn't stop thinking about tomorrow—tomorrow when Linda would be gone. I needed to think about today, a whole day spent with Linda on our way to the ferry at Northport, and tonight, a whole night to hold her and make love.

That didn't happen in West Fork. My cozy house had too many cozy neighbors for us to even consider it as a place to be alone. We dashed in and out on occasional errands, but a brief exchange of Christmas presents last year was the only one of our visits to my house that lasted any longer than five minutes. Instead, we followed the stereotypical dating pattern of a 1950s sitcom: one night a movie in Saukdale; another evening supper at her parents' house; some Saturday afternoon shopping in Spenceville; and so on. We presented the appearance of boyfriend and

65

girlfriend. We felt the reality of so much more.

My old green Falcon seemed to pull into the driveway at the Brays' farm almost of its own accord, as if conditioned by the daily routine of last summer. And just like last summer, Linda had watched for me out the front window. The door of the farmhouse opened as I made my way up the front walk.

"Hi," she greeted me in a subdued voice.

Her father emerged behind her carrying the small canvas bag that constituted her luggage. It must have been hard to play the all-American dad to a daughter with Linda's slightly counter-culture idiosyncrasies. I felt Don Bray would have been much more comfortable with a sturdy Samsonite bag in his hands as he sent his daughter back to school. It might have eased the tense creases in his face.

Helen Bray stepped out of the house last. She smiled at me. It was a real smile, as honest and genuine as the rest of the country's image of forthright, rural middle-America. I didn't know exactly what Don thought of me, although it surely involved the word *less*, but things were different with Helen. I knew. I knew she liked me, and I knew she liked me in the most important way. She liked me with Linda.

"Good morning, Jim," Helen greeted me warmly.

I smiled back with a respectful "Good morning" of my own.

"It doesn't seem like we've seen enough of you while Linda's been home," she said while her husband stood by silently. "Here, I remembered you like homemade bread. I bake every Saturday morning, you know. You take this, and I want you to stop by once in a while on Saturdays and pick up a loaf. We surely don't see enough of you when Linda's away."

Helen was being her usual, gentle self. I never stopped by when Linda wasn't home, and even though Helen's bread tasted better than any I had ever eaten, the temptation to my stomach would not lure me out to the farm until Linda returned again. In fact, my stomach, and the churning feeling it experienced when I encountered Don, would almost certainly keep me away.

"Mom, we have to go," Linda said, embracing her mother. "It's a long trip, and I can't miss the ferry."

Linda had a ferry to catch but not for almost twenty-four hours. While we carefully kept our pretenses up, this mention of the ferry sounded more like an excuse to get away than a facade of false propriety.

"Can I take that bag, Mr. Bray?" I asked.

"I've got it." He headed down the walk toward my car. Don Bray rarely sought or needed another's help. He placed the bag on the back seat of the Falcon then stiffly held the door as Linda slid into the front.

"Drive carefully, Jim," he said with a touch of softness creeping into his voice, a bit of emotion surely meant for Linda but directed through me.

In the past ten months, I had learned to let Linda speak first about things between her and her father. In these cases, the natural reticence within me, a trait that often exasperated her, became an ally. We left the gravel and drove almost halfway to Saukdale before she was ready to talk.

"It's a gray day," she said in a tone gloomier than the dreary, ash-colored clouds covering the sky.

"Sometimes, I like driving together on a dark night or a day like this," I said. "I feel closer to you, like it's just the two of us all alone with the rest of the world blocked out. In West Fork, we can never be by ourselves that way. I never feel like it's just you and me, as close as we want."

"I know," she sighed. "I really know."

The resignation in her voice reached down deeper than my frustration about the inability to make a private and personal relationship more personal and still private in West Fork.

"Jim, we have to talk."

"About what?"

"I think . . . well . . . this is hard," she said.

I glanced at Linda quickly. Sadness settled into her eyes, and those deep piercing pupils had to see the apprehension rise in mine.

"No, Jim, it's not us . . . not exactly. It's this summer."

"Uh, okay." I gave an audible sigh of relief. "What about this summer?"

"I'm not coming home. It just won't work."

"Your dad?"

"Yeah, everything is just too hard. It starts with something small. It gets bigger and bigger, but it always ends with the war. He won't accept how I feel, and Mom always gets caught in the middle."

"Do you have to argue with him? Why not just let it go sometimes?"

"But it always comes up. I mean, don't you watch the news? Don't you read the paper? The war is there. Nobody can ignore it. Nobody should ignore it."

Actually, I didn't watch the news. I had the feeling that half of the families around West Fork turned on the news at suppertime and managed to spoil their meals together. I might have been alone, but I preferred silence to a television set ruining supper every night. I kept just well enough informed about Vietnam to know that I hated everything that was wrong and knew nothing about what was right. Wrong was easy. We were wrong. I was just as sure the other side was wrong, too. But right? Where the hell could somebody find right in all of it? I made tuna casserole, read sports magazines over my dinner, and turned on the TV for reruns of old westerns at six-thirty when the airwaves were safe from the nightly news.

"I thought you wanted to work for Doc this summer."

"I do but I'll never make it through the whole summer at home."

"But ever since I met you, you've said you want to take over for Doc some day. How can you do that from Michigan?"

"Don't you see? It'll be different when I'm on my own. If Doc can use me after I graduate, I can get a place for myself. I wouldn't live with my folks. Anyway, the damn war will end someday. It has to. We can't win a civil war thousands of miles away, and the American people won't put up with it forever. Not even you."

Linda knew how to push my hot buttons. And now, three little words had done it. I felt anger rise within me, but maybe she had to make me mad right now. Maybe it let out some of the anger she felt. In some ways, it didn't matter. She couldn't live at home again. Some equally simple words from her father to Linda, or her to him, would set them off. After all, she had learned about straight talk from her father. Maybe she learned too well. Maybe, also, Linda's last three words to me stung so hard now because they were true. I fixed my eyes forward and drove along our summer stretch of highway in silence.

If Linda most often had the last word between us when we were mad, she even more frequently said the first words to make it pass. She possessed the stubbornness to stay quiet an uncomfortably long time, but I had an even greater weapon in the battle of long silences. I never knew what to say. I could not even fall back on a torrent of righteous indignation because most of the time Linda was right. She was right today, and she was very upset. Her stubborn silence lasted less than five miles before she squeezed over close to me on the seat of the car.

"I'm sorry, Jim. It's not you. I wanted the summer with you. I want to work for Doc. I want to have my life back here, but right now, it just can't happen."

"Still, what are you going to do about a job and everything?"

"The vet school always has research projects. There will be lab work or something. I can probably even get some course credit for it and stay right in the grad school dorm as an enrolled student."

"What about us?"

"I'll still come home once in a while, and you can come up and see me in Laurel."

"Linda, I haven't been to Michigan A&E once this year. You haven't wanted me to come."

"It's such a long drive, Jim. I don't want you killing yourself in the middle of the night driving back from Michigan."

She always used this excuse. Actually, driving Linda halfway up Lake Michigan in Wisconsin rather than simply taking her to Laurel probably saved me three hours at the most. She could see the questioning look in my eyes.

"The summer will be different, Jim."

"Oh, is Laurel moving closer to Illinois for the summer?" I said.

"No, and Illinois isn't moving north, either. But it'll be light a lot later at night, and driving back to make dustpans will be a lot different than driving back to teach children."

"I don't know. Anyway, I wish we could have talked about this before, instead of you just telling me in the car."

"I didn't decide until last night. Besides," she whispered, placing a finger to my lips and laying her head on my shoulder, "I didn't even want to tell you now. I didn't want to spoil tonight."

July 4, 1970

"Hey, let's try this, Babe."

Dean Wilson looked over at Linda and pointed a long, skinny finger toward the sign that said Chub's Mirror Lake Inn. I had known Dean for less than two hours, the time it took to drive out of Laurel and up the west side of Mirror Lake. Already, I didn't like him.

Somehow, the drive Linda and I planned up the lake for a fireworks display this evening had become a double date with Dean and his girlfriend, rather his "old lady," Janet Tachynski. Jan and Dean were in Linda's group of theater friends from Laurel College. My introduction to the couple had begun with their overly cute, very stale jokes about surfer songs. Things went downhill from there.

It seems they rejected materialism including cars, "the classic American materialistic symbols." Of course, that left them somewhat landlocked in Laurel. I guess that was why Linda thought we should take them along, in my car, to see the fireworks. For the past forty minutes, Dean had punctuated the trip with asides about the lack of a radio in the Falcon. Apparently, anyone willing to be sucked into the materialistic values of car ownership should have possessed adequately refined aesthetic values to purchase a car with a radio for some music.

If I found Dean's comments about my car annoying, they didn't hold a candle to his easy familiarity with Linda. He could call Jan "Babe" all he wanted, but it seemed to me that Linda had a name. Now, he was walking toward the front door of Chub's Mirror Lake Inn with his arms draped around both women. Again, I figured he could restrict his attention to Jan. After all, they seemed to have taken very self-conscious care to let everyone know they were a couple. Both wore the same patched blue jeans, the same tie-dyed T-shirts, and the same long, dishwater blond hair. On the whole, Jan wore it all better than Dean. Her no-bra look certainly did more for the T-shirt. The fact that she apparently washed her hair on occasion also offered a nice touch that Dean didn't bother to emulate. I reached for the front door of the restaurant, and the threesome entered ahead of me.

Our arrival at five-thirty in the afternoon obviously placed us ahead of the normal crowd that I guessed would fill the place on a Saturday night. A bar topped with black Formica and a black, vinyl-upholstered bar rail stretched along one side of the room. Plush red carpet finished off the front of the bar, which was furnished with at least twenty bar stools upholstered in the same black vinyl. A gold-flecked mirror and rows of liquor bottles, probably chosen as much for their addition to the decor as the popularity of their contents, occupied the wall behind the bar. A single line of tables with red tablecloths and black vinyl chairs echoing the style of the bar stools filled the center of the long and narrow room. The wall opposite the bar held a string of booths, color coordinated with black Formica tops on the tables and red vinyl upholstery on the seats. Two color television sets, tuned to *Bowling for Dollars*, hung near the ceiling in diagonally opposite corners of the room.

"Hi, folks. Four for dinner?" came the greeting from the man behind the bar. His overall girth and round, chubby face left little doubt he was the establishment's proprietor. "Why don't you take a booth? Sharon will be right with you."

Seven or eight people sat at the bar with one eye on *Bowling for Dollars*. Couples with the good sense not to get involved in double dates occupied three of the booths. We settled into a booth near the back of the room, two places from the suspended television. A young woman about the same age as the four of us came to the table with menus and four smoke-gray glass tumblers filled with ice water.

"Hi, my name is Sharon. Can I get you anything to drink?"

"Do you have any herbal tea?" Jan inquired immediately.

"We have green tea or black tea," our waitress replied.

"Is it herbal?"

"I think it's just regular tea, ma'am."

"Well, could you ask?" Jan persisted.

"Sure," Sharon nodded, leaving the table.

I glanced at Linda, who studiously examined the menu while our waitress undertook the tea mission. Sharon returned from the kitchen in only a moment.

"It's regular tea, ma'am. Green tea or black tea."

"I guess I'll just have to have a Coke," Jan said with a sigh worthy of a theatrical performance.

Sharon took our remaining drink orders. Linda asked for an iced tea. Dean and I each ordered a beer.

"I'll let you look at the menus while I get your drinks. Our soup today is chicken noodle, and tonight's special is the sixteen-ounce prime rib."

"Sixteen-ounce prime rib," Jan piped up after our waitress left the table. "They give you half a cow and expect you to eat it all."

"I know," Linda said. "I'm not that hungry, myself."

I was beginning to lose my appetite, too, although Chub's menu had little to do with it. I looked at Linda and wondered how many prime rib dinners from her dad's cattle had helped put her through school.

"I may just have soup and a salad," Jan said as Sharon made her way back to our booth with four drinks on a tray.

"May I take your order?"

"Can I order soup and a salad?" Jan asked.

"Of course," Sharon answered.

"What kind of salad dressing do you have?"

"French, Thousand Island, Italian, creamy Italian, blue cheese, and red Russian."

"Do you have any yogurt dressings?"

"No, just the ones I said."

"Is your soup made from scratch?"

"Yes ma'am, we make all of our soups right here in the . . ."

"But does it come from a mix?" Jan interrupted. "I don't want soup made with a bunch of food additives."

"Our soup is made fresh, ma'am."

"Could you ask if it has any additives?"

"Yes, ma'am."

Our waitress returned soon with the bad news from the kitchen.

"The cook says he uses bouillon powder in the soup," Sharon reported with a look somewhere between embarrassment and exasperation.

"Oh, I guess I'll just have a cheeseburger. But no fries. I don't want any greasy french fries."

After all the cross-examination and two trips to the kitchen by our waitress, Jan had managed to order a cheeseburger and a Coke. Sharon immediately seized her opportunity to turn from Jan and take Dean's order. He asked for broiled whitefish and a baked potato, receiving an approving nod from Jan despite the transgression of selecting Thousand Island dressing for his salad.

"And what will you have?" Sharon said to Linda.

"I think I'll just have a shrimp cocktail and a dinner salad with vinegar and oil on the side."

"Good choice," Jan cooed toward Linda.

"How about you, sir?" Sharon asked, turning in my direction.

"I'd like a bowl of chicken noodle soup and a large order of french fries, please."

I could not remember ever ordering a bowl of soup and french fries for dinner, but it pleased me enormously at this moment. Linda looked much less pleased.

"*Muy listo,*" she whispered, while her deep black pupils fixed a stare clearly intended as a warning to behave.

In a moment of awkward silence at our table, I realized that the occasional background sound of voices at the bar had grown into a steady murmur, headed toward a low rumble. The ten minutes Jan spent shuttling our waitress back and forth to the kitchen spanned enough time for the regular Saturday patrons to begin rolling into Chub's Mirror Lake Inn.

"Hey, Babe, check out the bar."

Dean's vantage point from the opposite side of the booth gave him full view of the growing crowd that came to me only through sound.

"I figured they named this place 'Chub's' after the guy tending bar, not the people who come here to eat," Dean smirked.

I glanced over my shoulder and saw the bar nearly filled from one end to the other with middle-aged couples partaking of a ritual drink before dinner. Several of them presented ample evidence of the "middle" in middle age.

"Man, they're all wearing uniforms," Dean said.

Jan giggled.

"What do you call those shirts they're wearing?" he asked about the similar pullover shirts in various pastel colors that almost all of the men had chosen to wear into the hot July evening.

"Those are golf shirts, silly," Jan answered.

"Well, they don't look like golfers to me," Dean said. "They must all use carts because none of them look like they could walk around a golf course."

"At least you have golfers to look at," Linda chimed in. "All I can see is a bunch of people on TV throwing bowling balls."

"It's just *Bowling for Dollars*," I offered in response to the annoyance in her voice.

"Well, it's stupid. Look at that woman jumping around," Linda said.

"She probably just won some money," I said quietly.

"She acts like she just found the cure for cancer," Linda said. "I think I should be able to eat my dinner without watching a woman with a bowling ball acting like an idiot."

"Come off it, Linda. It really hurts you if those people have a little fun?"

My plain words and disgusted tone hung heavy in the air. Conversation stopped, and Linda's face flushed bright red as she looked down at the table. She made no reply to my blunt rebuke. I watched the crimson color rise in her cheeks and remembered a long ride from Saukdale back to West Fork one day last summer when a cat had left its mark on Linda's shoe. I knew this would be an equally long dinner.

July 5, 1970

I slipped the key into the door of our motel room. The fireworks over Mirror Lake had been spectacular last night, but later, for the first time since Linda and I had become lovers, we made no fireworks of our own. It is amazing how small a double bed can be when the two people in it don't want to touch. Now, I returned from breakfast, a breakfast eaten alone at the diner across the highway. As I opened the door, Linda stood, fully dressed, combing her hair at the opposite end of the room.

"Good morning." My simple words came tentatively. "I didn't know whether to wake you up for breakfast."

"That's okay. I'm not really hungry. Besides, I want you to take me someplace down on campus."

"It'll take me a couple of minutes to pack my stuff," I said.

"Can't that wait?" she responded.

"I guess so. We have to check out by eleven."

"The place I want to go isn't that far from here. Eleven o'clock shouldn't be any problem."

"But shouldn't we talk first? We ..."

"Not now, Jim," Linda said as she stepped toward me and gently placed her forefinger against my lips. "I'm barely awake. Let's just get in the car."

Though her soft touch should have been reassuring, the impatience to leave the room felt otherwise. Once in the car, we drove without speaking toward the campus two miles to the north. Only Linda's directions, guiding us toward her unidentified destination, broke the silence. We entered the campus area with little more than "turn left" or "turn right" having passed between us. As we curved along a narrow roadway marked Woodward Circle, Linda reached across the car and touched my shoulder.

"Here, Jim, pull into the parking lot on the left."

I turned the car into Lot 22. The sign restricted parking to permit holders from 7:00 a.m. to 7:00 p.m. on Monday through Saturday. A totally empty lot demonstrated the lack of any need to extend that parking regulation to Sunday mornings. The cluster of stone and brick buildings that stood on both sides of Woodward Circle showed no signs of human activity.

Linda stepped out of the passenger's side of the car and started toward a gray stone walk at the corner of the small parking lot. She walked slowly, waiting for me to reach her side, then gently grasped my hand as we followed the little walkway between two remarkably unadorned, cream brick buildings. The spot spoke of nothing but absolute ordinariness, and the portal formed by the walls of the two plain buildings hardly seemed the entry to any place that could promise even the slightest interest.

"These are Ag Chemistry buildings," Linda said in response to the puzzled look on my face. "Classrooms and offices are in one building. The other houses mostly labs. I think they were built about twenty-five years ago. Michigan grows a lot of flowers, you know, commercially. This is where the university tests fertilizers and stuff. Come on."

Behind the lab building, the path followed a long row of lilac bushes then turned to enter a square courtyard enclosed by tall, carefully pruned hedges on each side. Neatly mulched flower beds ran all the way around the courtyard bordering a small, central patch of green grass with edges trimmed so straight that they might have been cut with a razor. Clumps of green peony plants and iris beds mingled with brightly blooming knots of moss rose, petunias, bachelor buttons, and marigolds. Linda guided me to a decorative concrete bench at the far end of the courtyard.

"This is one of my favorite places on campus." Her voice rose with emotion beyond the simple beauty of the flowers. "There's nothing exotic here; no rare, beautiful tropical flowers like you find blooming in the greenhouse. This is where they test the plant food for common, everyday flowers. The kind people grow in their gardens."

"They're pretty," I said, perplexed and hesitant about the purpose of our visit here.

"I love it here. There's something so Midwestern about the place. It's like this garden holds a goodness you can sense and feel." Linda paused and clutched my hand tighter. "It's the same goodness you have, Jim."

Her last words came at me by surprise. A warm feeling spread through me like the warming sunlight that spreads over a perfect spring day, but no words rose within me to express that feeling.

"I'm sorry about yesterday," she said. "You came all the way from West Fork, and I made you spend time with people acting like jerks."

"I know Jan and Dean are your friends, but ..."

"Forget Jan. Forget Dean. I was the biggest jerk of all because I know better. Besides, they're not really close friends."

"But, I don't understand," I said.

"Jim, there are a lot of small things, good things, about the world that Dean Wilson will never know. He'll never even see them. But he helped me see one big thing very clearly, the war. At Laurel College, he's one of the anti-war leaders. I respect him for that. I respect him even at times when I don't like him. Believe me, yesterday I didn't like him."

"That goes double for me," I said.

"I know. Before you came up, I told them that we were driving up the lake for the Fourth. Dean asked if they could ride along. With everything he's done, I guess I would have felt kind of selfish saying no."

"Linda, I know how you feel about the war, but now it seems like the weekend's gone ... I mean everything's just taken away from us, and ..."

"You're right. It was more selfish taking our time away from you. I just felt pressured by Dean—by who he is. I may respect parts of him, but Jim, I love all of you. I love you so much more than you could know."

I tried to answer, but she folded her arms quickly around me and drew me into a long, tight kiss. We held each other close in the embrace of two lovers almost afraid to let go, afraid of the ease with which some other part of their worlds might slip between them again. Without breaking our embrace, Linda slid her lips to my ear.

"Aren't you glad I didn't let you check out of the room?" she whispered gently.

I was glad. Still, I smiled first at the thought that Linda had been way ahead of me as usual. My smile broke into a wide grin as we stood and started hand-in-hand back to my car.

November 25, 1970

I had come to enjoy the drive to Northport. The trip took six-and-a-half hours from West Fork, and of course, I was always bursting to meet Linda at the ferry. But, time passed quickly on the Wisconsin portion of the drive. The flat Midwestern prairie gave way to rolling hills in northern Illinois, and in Wisconsin a succession of picturesque little towns on small lakes or old millponds dotted the route I traveled. It also seemed like every town in the state had its own bakery with some ethnic specialty. I didn't know whether all Wisconsin towns were settled by dominant ethnic groups or if they just worked harder to keep ethnic traditions alive; but I had learned that taking a coffee break in a different town on each trip allowed me to sample Danish *kringle* one time, German *strudel* another, and so on through Norwegian *krumkake* and Bohemian *kolaches*.

Unfortunately, today was different. Rain blanketed the Midwest and fell steadily through every mile of the journey. Plum River Elementary School had dismissed at noon for the Thanksgiving holiday, and I knew that Linda would reach Northport on the ferry hours before I could make it there from West Fork. The sullen sky, soaking rain, and disappearing daylight had created a dull, gray landscape that muted even the prettiest towns along the route; and the press of time had eliminated the possibility of an ethnic bakery coffee break.

I had looked forward to this trip in part to surprise Linda with my new car, a blue Plymouth Duster complete with AM radio. Now, the big storm filled the airwaves with static so that even the radio provided no break in the monotony of the drive. I rode in silence most of the way, checking the reception occasionally only to find even more popping and crackling interference each time as the storm intensified.

In some ways, it was just as well to keep the radio silent. The newscast I heard leaving West Fork had already foretold a holiday weekend with more arguing about the war than giving of thanks. Listening to the radio would only remind me every half-hour of the bombing at Michigan A&E early this morning. I knew it was wrong for me to think about how this would ruin my time with Linda. After all, two firefighters died trying to control a blaze caused by the bombing. That was a true Thanksgiving tragedy.

Still, I thought about our long weekend and the Thanksgiving dinner planned at the Brays' farm. The news report said the building that burned down included a lab housing military research projects. Linda and her dad couldn't avoid arguing about Vietnam under the best of circumstances. The bombing of a military research project at Linda's university sounded more like the worst of circumstances for Thanksgiving at their house.

I had promised to meet her at six-thirty for a quick supper in the coffee shop of the City Center Motel. My watch read 6:42 when I pulled into the motel parking lot. Linda's early morning ferry arrived at two o'clock, but I felt pretty good about keeping her waiting only twelve extra minutes, given the incessant storm I had driven through all afternoon.

I pushed open the large plate glass door of the restaurant and anxiously scanned the booths lining the room, searching for Linda's familiar form. My trips to Northport always produced an edgy anticipation that slowly built in every muscle until it tingled just beneath my skin as the long drive neared its end. Now, that nervous energy reached such a peak that my eyes darted faster and faster over the scene without stopping to gather information. I knew the release from the emotions that built up within me all day would come only if my eyes slowed down enough to come to rest on Linda, yet the harder I tried to calm myself, the faster my glance bounced futilely around the room.

"May I help you?"

My rapid scanning of the restaurant put my sense of sight in total control of my attention. Now, my sense of sound seemed somehow in competition.

"May I help you?" a waitress in a light pink uniform repeated.

80

"Uh, I'm looking for a friend," I responded, more from reflex than thought. "I'm supposed to meet her, but . . . I mean . . . what I mean is she should already be here."

"We haven't had many people in today," the waitress said. "Lots of times it's slow the day before a holiday. What's your friend look like?"

"Her name is Linda," I answered then finally entered the conversation far enough to realize that wasn't the question. "I'm sorry. She's twenty-three, about five foot four with short brown hair and blue eyes. She should have a duffel bag with her."

"A duffel bag?"

"Yeah, she came over on the ferry."

"I think you should go down to the ferry office."

"Oh, she won't be there. She came over on the morning ferry. She probably got in about two or two-thirty."

"I think you should go down to the ferry office," the waitress repeated in a hollow but insistent voice. "That's definitely what I would do."

The young woman grabbed a coffeepot from behind the long restaurant counter and quickly headed off to serve her handful of Thanksgiving Eve customers. My emotions sank as I finally realized that Linda wasn't here. Maybe the waitress' advice did make the most sense. The ferry office was a place to start. If I had mixed up our meeting place, Linda would be getting nervous herself by now. I looked at my watch. It read 6:50, twenty minutes past our appointed meeting time. With a six-and-a-half hour drive back to West Fork still ahead, we needed to hook up soon.

It took only three minutes to drive to the ferry dock, yet in that time I entered a whole new world. I remembered the first time I picked Linda up from the carferry. I had pictured a sleek, double-decked hydrofoil gliding up to a flag-festooned dock to discharge comfortable sedans and station wagons full of families enjoying an excursion across Lake Michigan. How was I to know that "carferry" referred to railroad cars, and that Linda would arrive in a 400-foot freighter with its ungainly square stern brought tight against a set of railroad tracks ending at the water's edge?

I headed my new Duster down a wide roadway covered with cinders and gravel. The wooden planks of the railroad crossings offered their distinctive loose thump as I drove over three sets of tracks to the ferry office, tucked away in a steel-sided warehouse surrounded by the same cinder and gravel surface as the roadway.

81

The black sky, steady rain, and charcoal-colored ground merged into an inky shroud revealing little more than the shapes of the buildings occupying the gloomy landscape. The empty docking slip indicated that the ferry had long since unloaded its cargo of railroad cars and returned to Michigan. My visits to the ferry office had never come at this time of day, and the number of automobiles parked in front on a dreary late-November night took me by surprise.

Opening the office door reminded me that the big boats ran on schedules to suit rail cars, not passengers. Somber-faced occupants filled nearly all of the square-shaped chrome and vinyl lounge chairs in the waiting room. If all were passengers, they could expect an arrival in Michigan during those early morning hours normally reserved for deep sleep. Either the prospect of that nighttime journey or the gloomy night itself had cast a solemn silence over the room.

Somehow, I expected to find a grizzled old man in a frayed blue sweater selling tickets, but as I approached the counter, I saw instead an agent just about my own age. A skinny brown tie, white shirt with soiled cuffs, drooping shoulders, and tired eyes cloaked his slender frame with a forlorn air almost stunning in a person only halfway through his twenties. Could a job as a ticket agent possibly be so unpleasant or unpromising that it produced such an effect?

"May I help you?" he asked in a low voice intoning the same resignation carried by his appearance.

"I'm looking for a friend. Is another ferry due in soon?"

My question had leaped ahead to a new scenario for Linda's absence at our meeting place.

"No, sir, there are no ferries tonight."

"Well, I was supposed to meet someone who came over on the two o'clock ferry, but I missed her somehow."

"The two o'clock ferry did not come in, sir."

"You mean there were no ferries operating today?"

"No, sir, the two o'clock didn't arrive. It radioed a distress signal about an hour from port."

"What do you mean, distress?" I shot back.

"The ferry called in a mayday because of the storm, but we lost radio contact almost immediately. An ore boat in the area headed for the location. They didn't make contact or a sighting."

"But . . . but the people . . . the people on the ferry," I stuttered and struggled for words as shocked confusion rattled in my head.

"The Coast Guard initiated a search immediately. I'm sorry, but nothing could be confirmed before it got dark."

"But the people. They're still searching, right? I need to know about Linda Bray. She was supposed to be on that ferry!"

"If she reserved a stateroom or a place for her car, I can check to see if she was onboard."

The clerk's hands shook visibly as he shuffled his lists.

"No, no. No. She never did that. No." I only wanted to say no, as if repeating the word could deny everything that was happening.

"Could she have paid by check?" the clerk asked. "The Michigan office also wired us a list of people who paid by check. What was her name?"

"Linda Bray," I spelled the last name and heard the letters come back to my ears with an empty, unreal sound. "B-R-A-Y."

The young ticket agent slowly turned his papers toward me. "I'm sorry. Her name is third on the list."

I stood in silent, paralyzed shock. Though the clerk spoke, I did not hear. Gradually, I sensed his words fading in and out almost like a radio signal fading in and out through the static of the continuing storm.

". . . can use this phone . . . it's for . . . pay long distance . . . company expense . . . if you need . . ."

"I don't know," I finally responded through my daze. "You're telling me the ferry sank? Weren't there any lifeboats? What about the people?"

"Sir, we do not have any confirmed information, but the Coast Guard did not sight the ferry or any survivors before dark."

Suddenly, the agent had used a different word. *Survivors.* Any *survivors.* I looked at the phone on the end of the counter. Next to it stood a tall, narrow candy machine with a rounded, streamlined top and long, thin chrome knobs sticking out almost like a misconstructed smile. I took a long look at the old machine and the chrome lounge chairs. This couldn't be right. This was 1970. Everything looked like 1950. This had to be another time. Or a dream. A terrible dream. Linda couldn't be on a ferry that sank.

My mind rejected the scene, but my body moved slowly toward the phone. My body knew. This was now. This was real. I dialed the long distance operator and asked for West Fork, Donald Bray.

"Hello."

"Mr. Bray?"

"Yes."

"This is Jim. Jim Blair. I'm in Northport. Something terrible has happened with the ferry."

My voice cracked as I began my explanation. On the other end of the line, Don Bray never wavered. In one minute, he gathered from me all the information I had struggled five times that long to comprehend from the ticket agent. The ferry, the storm, the mayday, the Coast Guard, Linda's name. His questions led to each piece of the story.

"Jim, I'm on my way to Northport. Can you get me a room there?"

"I don't think you should do that, Mr. Bray."

"Look, Jim, I don't have time to discuss this with you," he said in a firm, clipped voice. "I want to get to Northport as soon as possible."

"No, I think you should stay with Mrs. Bray."

Don Bray had spent four years earning distinction in the Navy, four years on big ships and huge waters. Now, I was telling him what to do when a big ship was missing, when his daughter, his only child, was missing with it.

After a long pause, I heard his voice change on the other end of the line, "Are you sure, Jim?"

I felt tears begin to well up in my eyes as I repeated softly, "I think it's very important that you stay with Mrs. Bray."

December 5, 1970

I reached for the door of the West Fork Store, wondering why I was there. The world around me looked the same, but my whole life had changed. Maybe I headed to the store this Saturday morning out of habit, or maybe I entered its front door just because it didn't make any more sense for me to be home. For the last ten days, no place made any sense to me; no place offered a real reason to be there. On Thanksgiving Day, the Coast Guard found a few pieces of debris and loose lifesavers near the ferry's last location. They found nothing more. The ship was lost with no survivors, no explanation. They could only report that it must have happened quickly. That quickly, my whole world changed.

I spent the weekend and the first two days after the Thanksgiving break at my parents' house. By Wednesday, returning to West Fork, to work, to my students, seemed the only thing to do. Now, like so many Saturdays before, I walked through the front door of the store to see the familiar faces of Bill and Margaret Dublin, Doc Shelby, and Wayne Mitton. Like so many Saturdays before—like no other Saturday before.

"Hi, Jim," Margaret said softly. "Sit down."

Without even asking, she moved behind the counter to pour a cup of coffee and put a chocolate donut on a paper napkin. As she placed them in front of me, I reached for a dollar in my pocket, but Bill touched my arm and gave a slight shake of his head.

"How are you doing, Jim?" Doc asked in a tone very different than that of any other Saturday morning.

"I don't know. Okay, I guess." I fumbled for words. "I made it through three days of school. I think being with the kids actually helped."

I drew a deep breath as Wayne Mitton spoke, "Are you going to the service, Jim?"

"No, it's going to be private. Just family."

"I knew that's what Helen wanted. I thought maybe with you and Linda so close . . ."

Wayne's voice trailed off as if his search for words ended in the same emptiness as the hollow place I felt inside me. Somehow, he knew about Linda and me. Of course, everyone knew we dated, but this was the first time I realized that everyone knew how much more there was between us. Did they know because of the time I took from work? Did they know because I was the one waiting in Northport for Linda on that terrible Thanksgiving Eve? Did they know just because people in little places like West Fork always know the truths in their neighbors' lives, even before those truths are spoken? After all, what greater truth can there be than two people in love?

"Did you take care of the cemetery?" I asked Wayne, already knowing the answer.

"I opened the grave yesterday and raked that spot as neat as a doorstep," he said. "I checked again this morning. I want everything perfect for Helen's sake."

"I don't think Helen could take anything more," Margaret sighed with glistening eyes. "First Linda and then finding Don like that."

The fierce Lake Michigan storm that took Linda away seemed distant and unreal in West Fork. Don was different. Don Bray took his own life. A single shot to the head. In his own barn. Where Helen found him. This was too close and too real. Don Bray's suicide shook the community even more deeply than the ferry accident that was its cause.

"I'm sure that's why she wanted a private service," Doc said.

"Don didn't have any brothers or sisters. I wonder who'll be at the funeral?" Wayne asked.

"Well, I know that Helen grew up a couple hours north of here. She still has a sister and some other family up there," Doc answered, "and Don had quite a few aunts and uncles and cousins over east of Spenceville. I remember he used to talk about playing ball against his cousins' teams."

"Boy, he was a ballplayer," Bill said.

"Darn right," Wayne nodded.

"A competitor, too," Bill added with a trace of a smile on his face. "You could see where Linda got her spirit."

The moment of fond memories gave way to a somber, awkward silence around the small table. Each member of my clutch of coffee partners looked down at the table without a word, aware of the pain that shot through me simply at the sound of Linda's name. Finally, the rattle of the front door broke the unusual stillness in the West Fork Store. We looked up to see Howard Miller.

In two years, I had come to like Howard very much. Even his remarkable habit of speaking in numbers only amused me. Launch into any conversation and Howard would manage to join in with little bits and pieces of enumerated data. Normally, the sight of Howard at the door would have brought a smile to my face. But not today. Today was different. My heart sank at the prospect of Howard recounting the number of funerals in West Fork this year, telling us the most points Don Bray ever scored in a basketball game, or worst of all, reminding me aloud that Linda was only twenty-three years old. I stood to excuse myself as the others began to exchange greetings with Howard. I added my hello and headed toward the door. As we met, Howard clasped his hands on my shoulders and looked straight at me.

"Jim, I know you're goin' through an awful rough time right now, and I think you should know what you mean to this town. I saw you with my boy, Andy, and I've watched you with the other kids. It's a big jump from that little Plum River Elementary School to the high school down in Sharon. But, the kids can tell that you believe in them, Jim. That helps a lot more than I'll bet you know. So now I think it's our turn to help. If there's anything I can do, or anybody in this town can do, you just ask."

I felt words catch in my throat as I barely managed to whisper, "Thank you, Howard."

I stepped to the door and outside. The cold air bit at my flushed face, but not even a strong December wind could cool the emotions burning within me. I walked home with tears rolling down my face.

May 22, 1971

A familiar cast of characters stood on the lawn of the modest white house where Doc Shelby's mother had lived. The twins were there. I didn't know anything about the two women, but I figured they must be in their mid-twenties. I had seen them at auctions before. They rarely spoke, even to each other; and the perfect duplication of their features, from the wavy brown hair pulled back with an elastic band to the pale, watery blue eyes to the sharp, slightly hawkish noses gave the twins an eerie, almost other-worldly air. They always bid on boxes of books and only boxes of books. Their quiet, cold resolve in this single-minded pursuit seemed to scare off other bidders. When they came to an auction, the twins went home with most of the books, usually at bargain prices.

Vern, from Vern's Antiques in Saukdale, would tell anyone who would listen that he never got any bargains at an auction. Despite that claim, he had appeared at each of the auctions I had attended during the spring. By his very bulk, no one could miss Vern. The white T-shirt he wore today had a long, yellow mustard stain from a hot dog just eaten, and the soiled garment failed to completely cover a stomach literally as large as the old-fashioned potbelly stoves an antique dealer might covet.

I saw Charlie wearing dirty, khaki-colored work clothes and a three-day growth of whiskers. I wondered how a person could always sport a three-day growth as Charlie apparently did. The stubble couldn't simply be trimmed to that length, so he must have shaved sometime. Since all the auctions I had attended took place on Saturdays, I decided that Charlie probably washed and shaved once a week on Wednesday—whether he needed it or not. I had no idea where Charlie came from; but I learned, as everyone else had, to keep an eye on him. He only bid on odd lots, those jumbles of tools, household items, and just plain junk piled together in cardboard boxes to make the auctions move faster.

Charlie had an unpleasant tendency to rearrange the contents of the boxes—before, during, and after the sale. I found this out the hard way at a farm auction a couple of months back when I got the bid on a box with a calendar plate for my mother's collection. I discovered too late that the plate had mysteriously moved to a different box that Charlie bought.

"All right now, boys, gather right around the wagon and let's see what we have here."

The raspy voice of Colonel Al Jorgenson directed the crowd as he and his brother-in-law, Will, climbed up onto a hayrack loaded with items to sell.

"What've you got there, Will?"

"A box of tools," Will responded, holding up the cardboard box and tilting it in the direction of the bidders.

"All right, boys, let's sell 'er all to go. What's my bid on the whole box?" Colonel Al shouted.

Al Jorgenson had to be well past seventy and for years had occupied the position as top auctioneer in the county. Now younger men did most of the auctions, but it was just like Doc Shelby to want Colonel Al. The Colonel always addressed the crowd as boys, even though women made up at least half the buyers at a household auction. He called everything he sold her or, more exactly, 'er.

Unlike younger auctioneers, Colonel Al never carried a portable microphone. To conduct an auction, he relied on only his voice and a loud clap of his hands when each item sold. That's the way he had always done it, but now, the wear of fifty years of hard use could be heard in that voice. Colonel Al struggled to make the sound of his words reach the back fringes of the crowd, and white flecks of spittle gathered in the corners of his mouth as he strained in the effort.

"Do I hear fifteen bucks on the tools? How about ten?" the auctioneer prodded. "Okay, five and go. Do I hear five?"

"Yes!" Will shouted, pointing to a raised hand at the left of the crowd.

"I have five," the Colonel responded. "Do I hear ten? I've got five now ten, five now ten, let's hear ten. Come on now, boys. Will, show 'em what's in that box."

"We got a set of three screwdrivers here, a good set," Will hollered, waving a small plastic case.

"I'll tell the world that's a good set of screwdrivers," Colonel Al called out. "What else do we have in there?"

"Here's a real nice hammer."

"Is that the kind with the one-size-fits-all handle?" the Colonel asked.

"I believe it is." Will laughed on cue at the joke he must have heard five hundred times before.

"Okay, boys," Al Jorgenson chided, "I've got five dollars. We're way low here. I'll take 'er a dollar at a time. Do I hear six?"

"Yes!" Will shouted as the bidding started again.

The bids came rapidly as the old auctioneer pumped a fist at each one-dollar increment. A clap of his hands signified that the box of tools sold at twelve dollars.

A clerk on the wagon handed a sheet of recorded bids down to me from the hayrack. Doc had asked me to help out today because he knew I sometimes attended auctions. Early in the morning, I worked with a couple of kids recruited by Colonel Al to set out the goods for the sale. Now, I was running the recorded bids from the clerk to a cashier's table in the garage. Even this simple task gave me a different perspective on the amount of effort that went into an auction.

Before today, I went to sales mostly for the lunch stand and an excuse to lounge in the sunshine on a warm spring day. I might bid on a couple of small items, but the highlight of the day was usually a barbecued hamburger sandwich and maybe a piece of sour cream raisin pie. It was the food that brought me back to auctions. Maybe it was also the people. Sometimes, I still felt so damned lonely. On a day like that, just standing in the sunshine with a group of people, even people like Vern and Charlie and the twins, helped the loneliness.

"Jim, sit down for a minute," I heard a familiar voice say. "Al's grandson can run those sheets from the clerk for a little while."

Doc Shelby motioned me to a spot on the back steps of his mother's house.

"If my memory serves me right, this is your fourth year coming up, teaching in West Fork," Doc said.

"Yeah, I started in the fall of '68."

"Well, you seem to like it here. You know people here like you. Do you see yourself staying awhile?"

"I don't know, Doc. I'm not too good at making plans. I like the kids. I like

90

having them for both seventh and eighth grade. You see them grow up a little, and you want to be there for the ones coming back, you know, from seventh to eighth."

"That's good to hear. It's nice to know you feel that way."

In truth, I might not have known myself how I felt until I heard the words come out of my mouth.

"Jim, I want to talk to you about this house. Ten years ago, after my dad passed away, Mom moved over here from Iowa. My sisters and brothers are spread all over the country, and it just seemed best if Mom lived close to somebody. Anyway, I bought this house as a place for her to live."

"I didn't know that, Doc. I guess 'cause your mother was here when I came to town, I just always thought she'd lived here as long as you had."

"No, I bought this house to bring her over here. You see, I actually own the place. So it's not in her estate. When this auction's over, I have to think about what to do with it." Doc put his hand on my shoulder. "I'd like to sell it to you."

"Oh gosh, I don't know. I mean that's not anything I ever thought about . . . you know . . . a house."

"Listen, I'm not looking for an answer today," Doc said. "But, I wish you would think about it. I don't have to put the house on the market right away. Mostly, I wondered if you wanted to stay in West Fork."

I could tell from Doc's tone of voice that he wasn't just talking about being a teacher at the Plum River Elementary School. He knew that living in West Fork meant that I lived close to a lot of memories. Of course he knew. He must have had his own memories. Linda grew up wanting to be a veterinarian. She grew up wanting to be just like Doc Shelby.

"It's hard some days," I said. "Time helps, but even without the hard days, I've never thought about a house. I mean a house would take a down payment and other stuff I probably can't swing."

"Jim, I own the house free and clear. We could set up a contract, but that's not the main point. Think about whether you want to stay in West Fork awhile longer. I know you're wanted here. The house could be good for you. Anyway, we can talk about this again. Right now, let's get a piece of that pie before they sell it all."

January 19, 1972

"Jim, do you want another cup of coffee?" the cheerful voice called from the kitchen.

"No thanks, Connie. I'm fine. Everything was great."

Connie Rupp had invited me to her house for dinner once a month since the beginning of school, and every meal had been great. Tonight, however, she outdid herself, from the egg lemon soup to the shish kebabs to the homemade cheesecake. It still felt funny to call this place her house. After all, I had lived here for four years, though this room never looked as good as it did now with Connie's needlepoint, macrame, and hanging plants decorating the little house. Connie started teaching third and fourth grades at the Plum River Elementary School this year when Sylvia Anderson retired. After Doc prodded me into becoming a homeowner, it worked out perfectly for Connie to rent my old place from Irene Mitchell.

"I'll just be a minute more," Connie called again. "I have something to show you."

"No hurry. I'm just gonna stay comfortable and lazy right here on the couch," I answered. I did feel particularly comfortable and content tonight. This was a special treat, an invitation to dinner two weeks in a row. For half a year, Connie had invited me to dinner once a month, always on the second Tuesday. She told me the dinners were a way to say thank you for helping her through the trials of her first year of teaching. Inwardly, I blanched at the idea of anyone seeing me as either an experienced hand in the classroom or a source of wise counsel. I knew how much I didn't know. Still, Connie always came to me on her bad days, and she said it helped.

She picked out the second Tuesday of each month for dinner because of John. Connie and John already had their wedding date set, June 23, 1973, three weeks after John's scheduled return from a two-year stint in the Peace Corps. Every second and fourth Tuesday of the month, he traveled fifteen miles from his village to the nearest telephone and called her. She decided it would be proper to have me come over to her house if I could meet John by phone. In her mind, this long distance introduction would reassure him that I was just a friend.

I became part of Connie's second Tuesday routine, a routine planned around John's phone call. We ate supper at seven to ensure plenty of time for a leisurely meal before his call at eight-thirty. While they talked, I went to the kitchen and washed the dishes. Halfway through the conversation, Connie always put me on to say hello.

Somehow, it worked. The first time we talked, I told John, mostly to be polite, that I looked forward to meeting him. Now, that had become the truth. I wanted to put a person with that pleasant voice from half a world away that willingly talked to a total stranger because it seemed the best thing to do for Connie. I had already circled Connie and John's wedding date on the back page of my bank calendar, the section that always prints three years at a glance.

The Tuesday phone calls never lasted more than twenty minutes. The cost of overseas phone service dictated that. By nine, Connie switched on the TV and sat down next to me on her sofa to watch *Cannon*. She always sat close after the phone calls. I suppose she sat too close, but such a small impropriety seemed a very slight indulgence in the face of the very big loneliness that hanging up the phone had to bring. After the first second Tuesday, I never felt uncomfortable on the couch with Connie.

"That wind is cold tonight, isn't it?" she said with a shiver.

"I'll say. I really felt it walking over to the school today," I answered. "For once, it made me pretty glad West Fork is so small."

She smiled and walked past the couch toward the thermostat on the opposite wall. Apparently, the knit slacks and sweater she wore had failed to warm her up from the day's chill. They did conform to her body in a way that defined her figure much more clearly than the loose sweatshirts and dungarees she had always favored for our informal dinners.

My mother would have called Connie's build "sturdy," but tonight that description missed the mark by a lot. Her full breasts and round hips were not exactly news to any man with normal eyesight, but she rarely wore clothes that allowed her body to be appreciated so completely. Connie, I discovered, could look sexier than I ever realized; and I enjoyed looking at her more than the boundaries of our friendship should have permitted. As she fiddled with the thermostat across the room, I stole an extra long look at her, hoping at each instant that her pose would last just a little longer.

"I hope you don't mind," Connie said, turning and causing me to quickly avert my eyes. "This is something I wanted you to look at."

She walked across the room carrying a small notebook that she had taken from the stand holding the television set.

"I'm kind of nervous, Jim. You know that what you think means a lot to me. I don't know whether to do this."

The slight tremble in Connie's voice somehow made words temporarily escape me, and she spoke again before I said anything at all.

"What I mean is . . . uh . . . I do things to express myself. You know, like cooking or quilting or macrame. Sometimes, I like to write poetry. I write it just for myself, mostly. Just to express myself."

"I think that's good," I said in a lame effort to find my way into the conversation.

"Jim, I don't think you understand," she sighed in disappointment. "It's not that easy to show another person something that's really important to you. What I mean is, I don't need you to tell me that poetry is a good thing, like I'm one of your eighth graders."

Connie had moved through nervousness, disappointment, and annoyance in rapid order. I managed to stay stuck in confusion, a confusion she finally seemed to recognize. Connie sat down on the couch and drew up close to me. She held out her hand and rested the small notebook on my leg.

"I have a poem in here I'd like you to read. I think it's better than others that I've written. It has more meaning than some of the others, or at least it does to me."

"Sure, I'd like to read it."

She reached over and turned the pages, stopping in the middle. The lined page held a short poem in her distinctive, neat handwriting.

Two Lovers
Brushing cheeks they slowly bent together,
Her gentle touch closing around the stem.
He ran his finger along the dewy petals,
The scent of nature rising in the air.
Then joining loving hands below so softly,
They picked the wild flower for their own.

A stillness enveloped Connie's living room as I held the notebook in front of me. I kept my eyes fixed on the handwritten page, and my suddenly heightened senses felt her eyes fixed as steadily on me. In the stillness, warmth spread through my body. With each breath I took, I felt my chest rise and fall in perfect counterpoint to the whisper of Connie's breathing. Silence lingered in the air until the unexpected ring of the telephone put a startling end to the quiet.

I suppose I heard Connie answer the phone, but my thoughts stayed riveted to the written words before me. Only when her voice raised with a sharp "Oh, no" did I find my attention torn away from the poem. For an instant, I resented the intrusion, but that resentment faded quickly as I listened to the concern in Connie's voice.

"How bad is it?" I heard her say. "Are you sure? I have to do something. Isn't there some way I can call?"

I struggled with no success to make one side of the phone call into a full story. I knew only that the call was bad news, news that made Connie forget for the moment that I was even in the room. When my presence did register with her, she quickly turned to the wall as if to shield her conversation or even shut me away completely.

"What's wrong?" I asked as Connie finally hung up the phone.

"It's John," she answered with glistening eyes.

"That was John?"

"No, he's sick. John's in the hospital."

"Oh God, Connie, what happened?"

"His mom said dysentery. He got really sick, and they had to take him to the hospital. She said it was twenty-five miles from his village. I'm really worried."

As I stood up, Connie pressed against me and began to sob on my chest. I searched for words, but she spoke first.

"Jim, I have to do something. I just don't know. Here I am and it's so far away."

"Hey, shh, come on now. They'll take care of him."

"But I feel so guilty. He doesn't have anybody there. I've got to do something, and I can't even call. I can't really do anything."

"Look, his mom said he'll be all right, didn't she?" I said, softly stroking Connie's hair.

"But he's in the hospital all alone and I don't even know how . . . how even good it is. Or . . . or the doctors. Oh, Jim."

"Here," I said, sitting Connie down, "why don't you write him a letter. We can send it airmail, first thing in the morning."

"Just a letter? He needs somebody with him."

"I tell you what," I interrupted gently. "Write the letter and send a piece of yourself with it. Send John your poem."

I placed the notebook in Connie's hands. She turned her head toward me, and hints of relief and solace began to show in her eyes.

"Do you want me to stay awhile?" I asked.

Connie simply shook her head. She had a letter to write, and I had a short walk home on a cold January night.

March 4, 1972

"This is our chance," I said to the circle of young faces gathered around me in Saukdale's Fairwoods Junior High School gymnasium. "Go out and make the most of it. On defense, remember, set up a one-two-two zone. These guys are big. I want the four of you in the box to get a body on somebody and block them off the boards. Billy, you crash in from the point for the rebounds. Remember, Billy, you've got to be aggressive."

If life requires each day a full quota of little absurdities, I had just made my contribution by telling Billy Kimball to be aggressive. Billy took his place on the floor; and within twenty seconds, he started the second half of the Seventeenth Annual All-County Junior High Basketball Tournament championship game the same way he had begun the first—by scoring a basket. The shot tied the Plum River Rangers and Fairwoods Eagles at eighteen points apiece.

For three years in a row, the Plum River Ranger teams I brought to the all-county tournament lost in the first round, but this year was different. This team was special. Billy Kimball made it special. Billy dribbled, passed, rebounded, played defense, and did it all better than any of our other players. Even more than all that, Billy scored. Boy did he score, and in junior high school basketball, a team with a kid who could score like Billy wins ball games. Going into this championship game, our season record stood at 13 and 2.

97

Billy had help. Chuck Peterson, in the eighth grade like Billy, played center and he knew how to rebound. Craig Jensen was a seventh grader and a steady outlet at guard for Billy when other schools double-teamed our star. At forward, Tom Conley, my third starter from the eighth grade, was as controlled as Billy was flashy, as reflective as Billy was decisive, as steady as Billy was spectacular. In a game, Tom always positioned himself in the right spot; always stayed alert on defense; always scored 6 to 8 points; and no one ever called him Tommy.

Since the first week of February, CJ Martin had started at the other forward. CJ's brother played there last year before graduating to high school. As a sixth grader, CJ knew far too little about basketball to start at guard. Measuring only 4'6" tall, CJ stood much too short to start at forward. Even so, he hustled like crazy, and good things just seemed to happen when he played. I didn't need any more basketball logic than that. I started CJ, and I started him at forward. Besides, I wanted Billy at guard. I wanted the ball in his hands as much as possible. So Billy, our tallest player at 5'9", played guard. As the third quarter approached its end, the strategy of putting the ball in Billy's hands kept us in the game.

"Great shot!" I yelled as he drove to his right then swished a jump shot from the side of the free throw lane. "Now defense, everybody, defense!"

My shouts of defense provided only limited support to the five Plum River Rangers who faced the realities of trying to stop the tall Fairwoods team. They were big, huge really, by junior high standards, with three kids over six feet tall. Even so, I was glad we were playing Fairwoods. Despite their size, despite playing the tournament this year at the Fairwoods gym, despite their reputation as the best coached and most disciplined team in the county, I was glad we were playing Fairwoods. We could have faced McKinley, Saukdale's other junior high school, in the finals. For all of the size on the Fairwoods team, we could do one thing they couldn't. We could put the best player on the floor. Billy Kimball's talent topped anyone Fairwoods had on their team, but not so for McKinley. McKinley had Calvin Wyatt.

At 6'3", with strength and athletic grace beyond his years, Calvin Wyatt played with a determination equal to Billy's and a level of skill rarely seen in junior high. Fairwoods had lost to McKinley twice during the season, but Calvin's cousin, who started at guard, was hurt for the tournament. With the absence of his quickness and passing ability to feed Calvin the ball, Fairwoods used its height and its disciplined pace to beat McKinley in the semifinals. We had no corresponding weapons to hold Calvin in check. The 38 – 37 Fairwoods victory saved us from a matchup where McKinley's ace could have trumped our ace. Against Fairwoods, we at least entered a game in which we held the high card, if not the best hand.

"Keep boxing out on rebounds!" I shouted from the sidelines.

Despite my exhortations, one of the tall Fairwoods frontline players put back a rebound for a basket. As the buzzer sounded bringing the third quarter to a close, the scoreboard read Fairwoods 32 – Plum River 28.

"Our offense looks good," I said to the team huddled around me between quarters. "Stick with the same setup and take the open shots whenever you get them. Chuck, keep setting those good picks for Billy, just like you've been doing. Ronnie, I want you to go in for CJ and block out on those boards."

Ronnie Harper had started at forward for our first nine games. Ronnie had grown sooner than the other kids his age; and for most of his school years, he had been taller, heavier, and stronger than his classmates. Now, by eighth grade, other kids had caught and passed Ronnie. The weight that once made him more powerful than other kids only made him slower in a game like basketball. Ronnie had to feel the frustration of a world reconfiguring itself around him until it transformed him from the big guy into a kid of average height who carried around too much weight. Both the frustration and the slowness showed in the number of fouls he committed on the court. Still, he measured more than a foot taller than CJ, and Ronnie could put his bulk to work boxing out for rebounds. That might help keep us in this game.

We broke the huddle and the Plum River Rangers took the court with one quarter left, one quarter for the smallest school in the tournament to grab a championship away from the largest. As the two teams lined up around the center circle, every detail of the scene emphasized the difference in size between the two schools. Our four-year-old, gold jerseys with blue numbers looked less than plain next to the shimmering green uniforms with white piping, numbers, and falcon insignia worn by the Fairwoods team. Among the starters, only Billy stood as tall as the Fairwoods player matched against him. Down the sidelines, ten reserves, all eighth graders, sat in waiting if needed by the Fairwoods coach. Five kids, a mixture of sixth and seventh graders, sat to my right comprising the Plum River bench. I wondered if I alone noticed these details.

Across the gym in our section of the bleachers, I saw Art Kimball, Tom Martin, Paul and Sharon Conley, the Petersons, the Harpers, and all the team parents. Connie Rupp sat next to Doc Shelby in a string of adults perched above a sea of young faces representing almost every grade in our school. In that whole cluster of people, filling almost a quarter of the stands, I read not a single expression of concern. Their eyes, smiles, and bobbing heads spoke of a moment filled with too much fun and anticipation to leave any room for concern.

A chorus of shrill screams, at a pitch possible only for pre-teen girls, accompanied the toss of the ball for the center jump. Using their height, the Fairwoods team controlled the tap and moved the ball slowly into the frontcourt. Three of their players began to pass the ball methodically around the outside of our zone while the two biggest kids worked in equally deliberate fashion for position close to the hoop.

The team in green and white patiently moved the ball, fully aware that its four-point lead allowed the luxury of holding possession until we loosened our tight zone. Their patience suited me fine. The longer we stayed within four points of the huge Fairwoods team, the better opportunity we had to pull out the game at the end.

Nearly a minute ran off the clock as Fairwoods demonstrated the style it had used to beat McKinley Junior High and Calvin Wyatt. The big team's play embodied its well-earned reputation for discipline and coaching. That Fairwoods could even point to a reputation represented yet another difference between a school as big as theirs and one so small as ours. Small towns and small town people rarely earn notice, much less reputations, in bigger places.

Although Billy Kimball had already scored twenty points, Fairwoods still seemed to regard him as just another player. In the fleeting moment of one pass thrown too slowly, Billy jumped out of the zone for a deflection. Just as quickly, he gained control of the loose ball and headed down the court. His breakaway layup brought the Plum River rooters to their feet and the score to 32 – 30.

Narrowing the lead to a single basket forced a change in the Fairwoods strategy. Three quick passes and an exchange of positions across the lane by their post players brought the ball inside. As the Fairwoods player went up for his shot, Ronnie Harper arrived with a crash. Though a step too late, Ronnie's weight and momentum knocked the shooter off balance. The shot banged off the rim, but the referee's whistle sent Fairwoods to the free throw line for two shots. The first of the pair bounced long off the back of the hoop. The second free throw found its mark.

Tom Conley inbounded to Billy who moved the ball back up the court. Billy passed to Chuck Peterson then received a quick return at the top of the key. Without hesitation, Billy dropped in a twenty-foot shot bringing us to within one point.

Fairwoods took possession. With little wasted motion, their deliberate passes moved the ball inside again and answered Billy's shot by scoring from within the lane. Now, the teams traded baskets each trip down the floor. Fairwoods found no defense to hold down Billy, and we had no defense against their size. I looked at the clock with each possession, watching the time fade away in this trading game. With forty seconds left, I called timeout.

"Okay guys, let's have Billy bring the ball up and clear out the right side for him. Everybody understand what I mean? Billy, get the best shot you can. Craig, go to the other side of the key as an outlet. If they double-team Billy and he throws to you, then you take the shot. When we score, set up in a man-to-man press. We need a takeaway. Try for a steal before they can throw it down low again." I paused for a quick breath. "Be aggressive. If we foul trying to get the ball, they still have to make the free throws. That's better than letting them get the ball inside. A foul won't kill us. Everybody understand?"

Billy received the inbounds pass, and not a single Plum River player stood on the right side of the lane as he crossed the ten-second line. Still, the Fairwoods coach was not about to let Billy Kimball beat their team single-handed. Two players in green and white stepped forward to meet Billy with a double-team. They moved toward him then hesitated for an instant.

In that moment, despite wearing the shimmering uniforms, despite playing for a much larger school, and despite standing much taller than their opponents, the Fairwoods players demonstrated they were still junior high kids. For a split second, the shared responsibility to guard Billy resulted in neither Fairwoods player taking decisive action. That provided all the opening he needed.

With a quick dribble, Billy sliced between the defenders and headed toward the basket. Driving down the lane, he looped a shot over the Fairwoods center, scoring the basket and drawing a foul in the same motion. Stepping calmly to the line after the foul, Billy dropped in the free throw for a three-point play. His twenty-ninth point of the game tied the score with sixteen seconds left.

Like the cheering fans across the gym, I jumped to my feet to celebrate Billy's shot. Only after Fairwoods put the ball in play did I realize that I had become too much a fan and not enough a coach.

"No press, no press!" I screamed, too late to get my team's attention.

Our press was already in place. Suddenly, I remembered the rest of my timeout instructions. With the score tied, committing a foul really could hurt us now.

"No fouls, no fouls!" I yelled, too late again.

With only four ticks gone off the game clock, Ronnie Harper reached wildly for the ball and collided with a Fairwoods guard. His fifth foul sent Ronnie to the bench and our opponents to the free throw line to shoot one-and-one.

"CJ," I said, turning to the bench, "go in for Ronnie. Take the top spot on the lane for the free throws and be sure to box out the shooter."

I absent-mindedly tousled CJ's hair as I sent him onto the court. He shot back a quick look of annoyance, one born no doubt of being the little guy who always got his hair tousled. No matter how big the game or crucial the situation, I guess a guy had his dignity to protect in front of all these people.

Number twenty-six for Fairwoods toed the free throw line with twelve seconds left in the game. His first free throw slipped cleanly through the hoop making that zipping sound in the net that only happens on a perfect shot.

With a one-point lead, he took his second shot in textbook form, sending the ball toward the basket with ideal rotation. The basketball gently touched the inside of the rim then spun around the perimeter falling almost straight down off the left side of the hoop.

All game long, the taller Fairwoods players had dominated the boards, scoring baskets in both halves on rebounds of missed free throws. This time, however, Tom Conley held perfect position on the inside rebounding slot along the lane. The Fairwoods center reached vainly for the ball as it dropped directly into Tom's hands.

Reacting before anyone else on the court, Billy Kimball moved immediately to Tom and took charge of the ball. He pivoted away from a defender and started his dribble. Billy could see me frantically waving to him to call a timeout. He coolly took the ball across the ten-second line then stopped to signal for time. The referees' whistles blew with five seconds left to play.

Ten kids, all talking at the same time, gathered in a huddle around me.

"Reserves step back," I barked. "Everybody quiet down."

Either my manner or, more likely, the situation got their attention immediately. Now, I just had to figure out what to tell them.

"Okay, okay. We've got the ball on the side here." I pointed in the proper direction more for my own benefit than that of my players. "All right, they're gonna be all over Billy. That's okay. Let's try to get him open, anyway. You three guys line up right on the free throw line. Uh, I want Craig, no Chuck, I want Chuck on this side. CJ, you be in the middle, then Craig on the other side. Right in a line, close together. Got it? Now Billy, you go down right underneath the basket, and Tom, you take the ball out. Billy, fake like you're going along the base line in this direction then come up and cut around Craig's side of the lane. Use that whole line as a pick. Cut around and come straight toward the ball. As soon as Billy gets open, you throw him the ball, Tom. Okay, let's break."

It hadn't even occurred to me to plan a second option in case Billy didn't get open. I was used to Billy finding a way to make things happen. I was sure he would get free, or at least I was sure he had to for us to win. Coming into the game, I knew we needed a super performance by Billy to have any chance. Thirty points in a junior high game, or any game, was a super performance. If Billy made one more basket, he would have thirty-one points, and we would win a championship.

The referee handed the ball to Tom. He gave it a sharp slap. Billy faked then took three quick steps and cut hard around the picks at the free throw line. Tom delivered a perfect pass. In one motion, Billy started the ball toward the floor for one dribble to square up with the basket. As he cleared for a shot, that single little dribble brushed against his knee. His hand darted quickly to regain control of the ball, but he succeeded only in spiking it away. I saw the look on Billy's face and heard a groan from Tom as we each watched the ball roll toward the out-of-bounds marked by the base line.

In despair, I barely noticed the gold jersey moving in my peripheral vision. Then, CJ Martin had the ball in his hands. With no wasted motion, CJ turned and gently arched a shot toward the basket. The ball seemed to move in slow motion, appearing to know it should fall short, if only because of the size of the shooter. I rose up on my toes with my body language trying to nudge the shot over the rim. The ball almost fluttered as it glanced against the metal hoop and fell silently through the bottom of the net. The buzzer sounded with both referees gesturing emphatically—the basket was good!

For five seconds, every movement on the court had fixed an indelible picture in my mind. Now, in the moments that followed, everything turned to a blur. The Plum River Rangers milled around the court hugging each other, their fans, and even me. One hug, stronger than all the others, brought my attention back into focus. I felt Connie Rupp's arms around my neck as she kept repeating, "That was great, Jim. That was great, Jim."

I smiled at Connie and felt Doc Shelby's hand pat my back. I searched deep within myself but could find no way to make words come. As the celebration swirled around me, I felt Connie's exact words more deeply than I could understand, or try to express.

That was great!

July 12, 1973

Thursday morning brought little to look forward to as I walked into the assembly room at Saukdale Metal Products. Actually, little to look forward to summed up most of my summer. So far, Connie and John's wedding, now almost three weeks past, had provided my one social outing since school ended. Even the ordinary diversion of watching church league softball took a nose dive this year when play switched from fastpitch to slowpitch. As the challenge in hitting the ball diminished, so did my interest. Now, I wandered down to the diamond behind the Methodist Church for a Tuesday evening stroll but rarely stayed more than an inning or two.

The house always presented some chore to be done, but the house had pushed me into this summer job in the first place. I didn't care to spend my days earning money to cover my new expenses as a homeowner and still be a slave to work around the house in the evenings, as well. When Doc convinced me I could afford a house, he must have looked at it from the point of view of a veterinarian's income rather than a teacher's salary. Sure, I could swing the mortgage, the taxes, the insurance. Then came the bigger oil bill, the larger electric bill, the broken latch on the back door, and a dozen other surprises anxious to eat up my paycheck.

In terms of my budget, I should have looked for something more than this part-time position at SMP. But, re-entry into the summertime job market after a three-year absence had caused me enough discomfort. I shunned the trauma of a more extensive job search and came back to the assembly room as a part-time, substitute worker.

"Hey, Teach, hurry up," one of my co-workers shouted.

The limited supply of summer work turned out to be only one of many changes at SMP. Piecework rates for assemblers had inched ahead two cents in three years. In return for this generosity, the company had rolled back the system of graduated vacation days based on seniority to a standard one week for everyone in the assembly room.

"Teach, I need another batch of wires, quick."

Two years ago, Saukdale Metal Products went plastic: plastic canister scoops, plastic measuring spoon sets, and rumor had it that a plastic snow shovel might join the proud line of metal shovels any day. Already, the company had dropped its metal canister scoops, and plastic made up sixty percent of the measuring spoon business. Since SMP did little more than add its label to prepackaged spoons from another supplier, work in the assembly room decreased accordingly. As a by-product of the new products, the number of workstations in the assembly room had dropped from eight to four.

"Hey, will you straighten those out better," a voice giggled, as I struggled with yet another tangle of wires for dustpans with handles.

The face of the assembly room had experienced an equally dramatic change in my absence. Gone were the crews of middle-aged farm wives, replaced almost exclusively by young women from Saukdale's Mexican-American community. Young Mexican-American men also filled three of the four handler positions in the assembly room, though incumbents in all of the jobs apparently changed frequently.

"Put some more on my rack, Teach."

A sour-expressioned personnel officer had hired me to cover the week of vacation for each of the four handlers. He could not tell me right away exactly what weeks I would work, but he guessed that I would have more than four weeks worth of employment. He had allowed that, "Nobody wants to work anymore, and half of these Mexican boys probably won't come back from vacation until they drink up all their money back home."

I assumed "back home" meant Mexico, although all of my co-workers as handlers turned out to be recent graduates of Saukdale High School. The first two handlers I replaced also returned as scheduled from vacation, either a sign of their reliability or an indication of how little time it would take to "drink up," or spend in any other way, all the money that could be earned as a handler at Saukdale Metal Products.

"Rosa loves Teach," a loud laughing voice said in a Mexican accent as a young woman at the workstation reached down to help me pick up a batch of wires I spilled as I hurried to reload the assembly racks again.

The loud voice belonged to Teresa Terronez, a woman about twenty years old. Teresa's tall, husky stature distinguished her from most of the Mexican-American women in the plant. Her heavy makeup and the huge, wild pile of curly black hair on her head only added to a remarkably imposing presence for a person so young. Whether or not her manner represented a conscious decision to match her physical appearance, I could not know; but Teresa had clearly developed a big personality. If something outrageous could be said, Teresa said it and everybody heard it. My first day back at the plant, Teresa found out I was a teacher, and I became "Teach" to her and to everyone in the assembly room. Though her last comment startled me, "Rosa loves Teach" was very tame stuff by Teresa's standards.

If Teresa startled me, she amused Toni. Of course, judging by her constant giggling, almost everything seemed to amuse Toni. She giggled when she talked, she giggled when she worked, and she certainly giggled at anything Teresa said. Toni was tall like Teresa but slender and very pretty. She knew it and, again like Teresa, always came to work in full makeup. The makeup did much more for Toni than Teresa.

Rosa Rios worked quietly alongside the two tallest women in the room. My experience coaching junior high school basketball gave me a pretty good eye for height. If Rosa stood five feet tall, it had to be on her tiptoes. She appeared to like working with Teresa and Toni, but Rosa's height represented only a mere beginning of the differences between her and the other two women. She had a deeper brown tone in her skin and, although not heavy, carried a roundness to her shape that contrasted to both the bulky Teresa and slender Toni. Much more than physical appearance, Rosa presented a quiet reserve to the world that was very different from her two co-workers. Always friendly, her quick and easy smile never fully erased the bit of sadness in her eyes.

Rosa bent down for a second handful of the wires I had dropped on the floor. I could no longer count the number of times she had helped me out to keep up with the pace necessary to supply the workstation that the three women shared. For each "Hurry up, Teach" from Teresa or giggle from Toni, Rosa reached up to straighten the wires on her assembly rack or offered a quiet "thanks." Now, as the bell rang for morning break, she lingered to help me untangle the knot of wires.

"Here, Teach," she said, "I'll put these on the rack."

"Geez, I really appreciate that," I answered. "I want to bring over some more handles and pans before I go on break."

She gave me a quick smile and continued to untangle the V-shaped wires. Rosa clearly understood that all week my breaks had hardly been breaks at all. I used them to get extra wires on the assemblers' racks and carry over more wooden handles, metal dustpans, and paper decals. This head start usually got me to lunchtime without falling completely behind. Of course, it transformed the fifteen-minute morning break into just enough time to run to the bathroom. Today, the dropped wires might have interfered even with that trip if not for Rosa's kindness. I appreciated her thoughtfulness even more because I knew it would only add to the teasing she got from Teresa.

I picked a batch of wooden handles out of a tall cardboard drum and arranged them with their screw-threaded ends all facing in the same direction. The relief of break time must have slowed Rosa's normally nimble fingers because she was just placing the last of the dropped wires on the assembly rack as I returned with my load of dustpan handles.

"Thanks again, Rosa," I said. "This really helps a lot."

"I know we keep you moving," she said with a smile. "I don't mind helping. Anyway, we can say something besides just hello."

"Yeah, I know. There's not much time here to talk."

"Not much at all," she agreed.

Rosa stood still at her workstation, but I knew I had to get back across the room to make stacks of dustpans.

"Do you want to get a drink after work?" I heard myself say the words before my mind completely organized, or perhaps even considered, the thought.

"Tonight?" Rosa answered.

"Oh, uh," I stammered, realizing that tonight was Thursday. Maybe a weeknight didn't make any sense. This wasn't exactly like going out for a drink after work with the guys. Come to think of it, I never did that, anyway.

"Well, I guess we have to work tomorrow," I started again. "How about tomorrow night instead?"

"That would be nice," she said. "Where should we go?"

"Well . . ." I searched for an idea, but I never went anyplace after work in

Saukdale. I saw a questioning look cross Rosa's face as she waited for an answer.

Finally, Rosa spoke, "Let's think about it over lunch."

"Yeah, that would give me a minute. I have to get some other things ready before break ends, but tomorrow is okay, huh?"

"It's great," she answered.

"Yeah, great," I repeated as Rosa headed off for what was left of her break.

July 13, 1973

I took a nervous glance to my left at the sound of the lobby door opening into Riley's Tap. Instead of Rosa Rios, I saw a heavyset man in a beige, sports coat enter and take a place at the bar. Rosa had suggested Riley's Tap and wanted to meet here at four-thirty. I cleaned up and changed clothes in the locker room at work, then spent most of the hour since quitting time trying to entertain myself in downtown Saukdale. I bought a pack of breath mints at the five-and-dime, stared at the magazine rack in the drugstore, and still wandered into Riley's Tap at four-twenty. The clock behind the bar now showed 4:36.

Riley's Tap occupied a small corner of the first floor of the Bradford Hotel. Its side door opened from the hotel lobby. Riley's front door faced Second Street. For years, the Bradford had been Saukdale's top of the line hotel. The marble floors, gilded mirrors, and deep upholstered chairs that greeted the public in its lobby signaled to generations of businessmen, political campaigners, and distinguished visitors to Saukdale that this was the place to stay. Of course, many of those guests arrived by train. Today, Saukdale could still boast of a busy freight yard, but the last passenger service had ended more than two years ago. Now, businessmen likely as not chose one of the new motor lodges on the outskirts of town rather than spending a night at the Bradford Hotel.

Riley's gained a reputation over the years for great sandwiches and continued

110

to do a brisk lunch trade among downtown workers. However, the once bustling Bradford offered few customers on a late Friday afternoon. Only three men sat at the bar, each with expressions as empty as the vacant barstools separating them. I wondered if that was what Rosa wanted, a place where there would be no curious eyes of co-workers or Mexican-American friends. I took in the heavy oak tables with sturdy joined chairs and the line of empty, high-backed oak booths that extended along the wall to the back booth I had chosen. There was little chance that we would meet any acquaintances here, nor would Rosa have to sort through a crowd of faces to find me.

The door to Second Street opened just as I began to ponder the three lonely patrons seated at the bar. I looked up to see Rosa, a different Rosa, stepping in from the outside. She often seemed so serious at work. Now, in a pair of tight blue jeans and a gleaming white blouse that accentuated her brown skin, she carried a lightness about her that I had never seen before. I stood up by the booth and waved across the room to her.

"Hi, Teach. Sorry I'm late."

"Oh, that's okay. I was just kinda relaxing, nursing a beer. Can I get you a drink?"

"How about a seven-and-seven," she answered without hesitation.

She slipped into the booth while I stepped across to the bar to order her drink. Glancing back as I waited for the bartender to mix Rosa's seven-and-seven, I couldn't help but notice how small she looked surrounded by the heavy oak booth.

"Here you go." I handed the drink to her as I returned and slid into the booth on the opposite side of the table.

"Thanks," she said with a pause for a small sip. "That's good."

"Here's to Friday," I toasted.

"Friday," she repeated. "I guess that means it's our last day on the same crew."

"Yeah, you're right."

"You're probably glad to be rid of us," she said, "especially Teresa's teasing."

"No, you guys were okay. It's just the darn dustpan wires that drive me nuts, you know, keeping up. You really helped me a bunch."

"Do you work next week?" she asked.

"No, the boss says it'll be two weeks before they need me again."

"That's too bad."

"Yeah, I could use the money, but at least the dustpans should be over by the time I come back."

"We're gonna miss you."

"I'll be back," I said. "Anyway, the heck with talking about work. Tell me something about yourself."

"That's probably as boring as work." Rosa smiled. "What do you want to know?"

"I don't know. Have you always lived in Saukdale?"

"No, I was born in Mexico."

"When did you move here?"

"Actually, my father came first," she said. "He got work in the railroad yard. Then, he helped get jobs for my brothers, Manny and Pete. My father lived here three years before he could bring all of us up from Mexico."

"So how old were you?" I asked.

"Eight."

"And you have two brothers?"

Rosa just laughed, "No! Two brothers? I have four brothers and five sisters."

"Wow, there's ten of you. That's, uh . . . different," I said, searching for words.

"I know other families bigger than that," she answered with a hint of defensiveness in her voice.

"No, I mean that's different from my family. I don't have any brothers or sisters. It must be something living in a big family."

"I guess. Some of my older brothers and sisters I don't really know very well. I'm the youngest by four years, kind of an extra; and having a big family meant we were pretty poor. That's why my father came here, for money."

"We weren't exactly rich when I was a kid, either," I said.

Rosa looked at me skeptically.

"We didn't actually have running water in the house until I was six," I continued.

"How far did you have to go for water?" she asked.

"Well, we had a pump out behind the house," I said. "And, you know, the little necessary building farther back on the lot."

"Oh, a pump and a little necessary building," she nodded. "You weren't poor, Teach."

I felt my ears warm with embarrassment as my attempt to spin a tale of poverty fell flat.

Rosa seemed to smirk ever so faintly then broke the awkward silence with her own question, "When you weren't carrying water, what did you do for fun?"

"Mostly, I played tricks on smart-alecky little girls," I laughed.

She laughed too, as we bantered back and forth, occasionally revealing an actual truth about our lives and ourselves. The clock by the door had moved from 4:45 to 6:15 when I finally took my eyes off Rosa long enough to look across the room. The three people at the bar had multiplied to a dozen or so. I realized I was hungry.

"Hey, would you like a sandwich or something?"

"That sounds good," Rosa answered.

I reached for a laminated menu card from a holder on the back of our table and turned it so we could both read down the long list of sandwiches, from the Bradford beef stacker to the Saukdale clubhouse.

"What sounds good?" I asked.

"Teach," Rosa said, "I think I just want a cheeseburger."

"Yeah, me too," I laughed. "How about some french fries?"

"I'll split some with you."

"It's a deal." I rose from the booth to put in our order at the bar.

Rosa's company made another twenty minutes disappear in an instant, and the white-aproned bartender brought two plates with cheeseburgers, a wicker basket of french fries, and a bottle of ketchup to our table. I lifted up the thick bakery bun and shook a liberal covering of the ketchup onto my cheeseburger. Rosa reached for a small crock on the table. She carefully spread brown mustard over her cheeseburger, then nestled two pickle slices on top.

"That's good," we mumbled in unison, then laughed, with our mouths full of the first bites of cheeseburger.

"How long have you worked at SMP?" I asked Rosa as we reached simultaneously into the basket of french fries.

"About two years," she answered. "Out of the bunch of girls that work there now, I was one of the first."

"Do you like it?"

"It's okay." Rosa shrugged. "Not forever."

"What do you want forever to be?"

"Who knows?" She shrugged again. "My mother thinks I should be married with at least two or three kids by now. I'm twenty-one and I'm sure my father wishes I would find some Mexican boy to get me out of our house and out of his way."

"You're not very big to be in the way," I kidded to lighten a conversation I inadvertently had headed in the wrong direction.

"You don't understand, Teach," Rosa said, missing or ignoring my cue. "I'm the youngest and I am in the way. My father is sixty-two. He doesn't need an old maid daughter. All he really wants is enough money to go back to Mexico and live okay. So the sooner I'm gone, the better."

"Well, I'm glad you're here with me," I said softly.

A haunting moment of silence hung over our table as Rosa twirled the straw in her drink.

"You must have to learn how to say nice things in teacher school," she said abruptly.

A blush passed over my face. Rosa began to smile again. We finished off our sandwiches and let the laughs creep back into our leisurely conversation.

Though Riley's Tap clearly didn't need our booth, I wasn't sure we could sit there all night. Finally, I looked across at Rosa and asked, "Would you like to catch a movie or something?"

"I'd rather be alone with you," she answered quietly.

Her words caught me completely off guard and without a response.

"Wrong answer?" she said.

"No," I hesitated, now thinking practically about the state of a bachelor's house with no company expected. "Uh, we could go to my place. It's about a half-an-hour down to West Fork."

"Someplace closer would be nice." Rosa looked at me intently, leaving no doubt about the meaning of being alone.

"That's okay," I said quickly.

I hoped she didn't have the Bradford Hotel in mind. Even with its heyday waning, I knew the amount of money in my wallet wouldn't swing a room here. I worried, as well, that the management might frown on young couples checking in with no luggage.

"I think I know a place," I finally said. I took Rosa's hand, and we headed out the Second Street door of Riley's Tap toward my car.

In five minutes, we reached the outskirts of town on the south side of Sauk-dale. For the first time in three years, I turned my car down McCoy Road. I remembered the Town's Edge Motel which had left a vague impression in my mind on those summer days when Linda and I passed it on the way to her job at Griffin's Pet Hospital. This evening, I stopped two blocks short of the pet hospital and pulled into the motel driveway.

Rosa waited in the car as I stepped into the small vestibule that served as the motel office. The sound of a television and the lingering smell of the evening's supper clearly signaled a mom and pop operation. As I closed the door behind me, a middle-aged man slipped through the curtain that separated the little office from the owners' living quarters.

"Can I help you?" the man asked in a routine manner.

"I need a room." My voice cracked as I felt anything but routine.

"How many people?" he asked.

"Two."

"One bed or two?" He leaned his elbows on the narrow counter that separated us and served as the registration desk.

"Uh, one would be okay."

"And how many nights are you staying?"

"Just one, uh, I guess."

The sequence of simple questions managed to unnerve me enough that the qualifying "I guess" just slipped out. Maybe I subconsciously stumbled over saying "one night" when I knew the length of the visit would actually be less than a full night's stay.

The motel owner slipped a registration form into a black plastic holder on the counter and handed me a pen. I started to write my name, then awkwardly transformed the Jim into Tim. Tim Johnson, I wrote on the top line. I silently congratulated myself that at least I hadn't chosen Smith for my alias. My smugness passed quickly as it occurred to me that I might have to account for both guests in the room. I squeezed a Mr. and Mrs. in front of the Tim Johnson and filled in the rest of the form with a concocted address from my hometown of Brenton, Illinois. The deception completed, I immediately wondered what I would do if he asked to see identification. With no plan of action springing to mind, I wondered further why I was registering under a false name in the first place. The motel owner slowly studied the registration card then rang up the room charge. I exchanged $13.45 for the key to room six.

"Room six," I said as I opened the door on Rosa's side of the car and took her hand. She walked with me to the room three doors down and smiled patiently as I fumbled to put the key in the lock. On the third try, the door opened. We stepped into the room without exchanging a word.

"I'll just be a second," Rosa said as she moved toward the bathroom door straight ahead.

My eyes scanned across room six at the Town's Edge Motel. A blond-finish, three-piece bedroom suite consisting of a bed, desk, and nightstand filled most of the room. A white chenille spread covered the bed. The beige walls, caramel-colored carpet, and matching highlight colors in the cotton print curtains gave evidence of an effort at coordinated decoration. Unfortunately, the tones selected, in combination with the blond, 1950s bedroom furniture, left only a wall calendar from the local fuel oil distributor and a cheap print of the Grand Canyon as spots of color in a relentlessly bland room.

Plain though the room was, the proprietor's care showed in the cleanliness of the carpet, curtains, and walls. If I couldn't afford the Bradford Hotel for Rosa, at least I had managed to stumble into someplace clean. I turned toward the window and pulled down the roller shade. A flip of the wall switch by the door turned on an overhead light. I heard Rosa's soft footsteps behind me.

"Hi," I said moving away from the window.

"Here we are," she answered with a nervous laugh in her voice.

I reached out and put my arms around Rosa. I bent slowly to kiss her. Slightly misjudging just how short she stood, my top lip brushed the tip of her nose before reaching her mouth. She had closed her eyes and now pulled back with a start. Eyes open, we both broke into a laugh at the misguided kiss and the awkward embrace created by the difference of more than a foot in her height and mine.

Rosa pulled me over toward the bed. We sat on the edge of the mattress and joined in a tight embrace and long, steady kiss. We lay back on the bed and pressed our lips even more tightly together. The world outside of room six melted away in the feeling of Rosa wrapped in my arms.

As we kissed, my hand slowly traced a path down the front of her blouse with a finger and thumb coming to rest near her waist. I fumbled unsuccessfully with one of the tiny plastic buttons on her pure white blouse. She pulled away and whispered, "Here, let me help."

Rosa lifted herself up to a sitting position on the edge of the bed. With her back to me, she unbuttoned the blouse and reached behind to unhook her bra. My eyes gazed steadily at the rich brown luster of her skin as she tossed aside the clothing without turning around.

"Are you going to join me, Teach?" she asked softly.

"Mm, hm," I murmured as I dropped my shirt on the floor.

I reached out and touched Rosa on the shoulder, expecting her to lay back

116

onto the bed. Instead, she gently leaned forward and stood up with her back still in my direction. She loosened her blue jeans and in one motion removed her jeans and underwear together.

I drew a deep breath, surprised at the suddenness in which she stood before me undressed. Without her jeans, Rosa's legs looked even shorter than I imagined. There was nothing slender or statuesque about Rosa, but I stared at her softly rounded hips with the feeling that no woman could be more sensual. She slid back onto the bed and looked over at me. Her small breasts lay like teardrops on her chest. I could feel her eyes watching me as I slipped my clothes off.

I lay close beside her, and we kissed and embraced again. Our bodies became one so easily that an extra thrill of sensation tingled through me. We lost ourselves in each other and her soft murmurs of "*si . . . si . . . si.*" As we lay together afterward, the sweetness of how Rosa made love left me almost embarrassed to speak.

"You probably don't think much of me, do you?" she finally said.

"Oh, no, you were great, Rosa."

"Not that," she sighed. "I mean you probably don't think much of me for going to bed with someone I hardly know."

I flinched slightly at the thought so far from my mind.

"I'm here, too," I answered.

"Things are different, you know, for guys," she said in a low voice.

The sadness in her tone penetrated my heart.

"Shh," I said. "What I really think is that you are a wonderful person. I'm sorry if I didn't show that."

"No. That's not it. That's not it at all," she said. "I meant me asking you and everything. It's just . . . well . . . pretty soon you'll be going back teaching. I've liked you all summer. I just didn't think there would ever be another chance, you know, with you and me."

"But you see, I like you, too. You were just smarter than me to do something about it."

"I don't know," she said. "I have to tell the truth. Partly, I just wanted to see what it would be like."

I saw a little of Rosa's smile return to her eyes, but she must have read the confusion on my face. Everything about the last few minutes told me this wasn't Rosa's first time.

"I mean," she said, answering my unspoken question, "what it's like to be with a white guy, a tall, skinny white guy. Do you know I can count every one of your ribs?"

I smiled as she ran her index finger along my rib cage. I had never known anyone so tender with another's feelings or so direct about her own. I pulled her closer to me and held her tight.

"Will you have to go soon?" she asked.

"I'd rather stay awhile, if you can," I answered. "The room's paid for. We could lay here and watch some TV or something, if you want."

"I'd like that."

After a quick kiss, I hopped out of bed and turned on the television just in time to hear the theme song for *Love American Style*. I adjusted the volume and turned toward the bed. Rosa had pulled back the bedspread and slipped under the top sheet. I slid under the sheet with her and held her in my arms again.

"So what's the verdict?" I asked.

"This show is okay."

"Not the TV, Rosa. How is it to be with a tall, skinny white guy?"

She kissed my cheek then nuzzled up against my neck.

"It was good," she said softly. "You were very good."

August 24, 1974

The six o'clock sun had dropped low enough in the sky that trees on the hillside began to shade the asphalt parking lot next to Our Lady of Guadalupe Church. Booths and decorations on all sides had transformed the space into a temporary courtyard, and I found a seat for myself at a long folding table covered with clean, white butcher paper. I put down my plate heaped with an enchilada, bean tostada, and beef taco all covered with mounds of shredded lettuce, diced tomatoes, and crumbly white cheese. If I finished all this food, it would surely take me the rest of the evening. One bite confirmed that the Saukdale Mexican Fiesta richly deserved its reputation for both the size and taste of its traditional meal. In reality, I had all night to finish my supper. I was alone and dependent on my own devices for the evening.

Looking from my table toward the back of the courtyard, I could barely catch a glimpse of Rosa working in the big tent that served as a kitchen. Our eyes had met as I passed through the food line, but that was all. She had asked me not to come tonight and relented only when I promised not to speak to her.

For more than a year, I had been the secret in her life and she the one in mine. At times, I talked to Rosa about changing that, but she felt the pressure of the cultural boundaries set by her family. I always claimed that those boundaries should not stand between us. Then, I just as consistently found it convenient not to push too hard. I stood on the high ground but managed not to dig in very deeply. Maybe Rosa sensed that I might let her challenge too many of those cultural boundaries alone.

"Hi, Teach," a familiar voice said just as I pondered whether I could possibly eat another bite.

I turned to confirm the identity of the person behind me, though it hardly seemed necessary. The loud, sassy hello had to come from Teresa Terronez.

"Hi, Teresa," I answered with a smile.

"You musta missed us from the factory, huh, Teach?" she laughed. "Did you have to come down here to see all the Mexican *senoritas?*"

If Teresa intended to embarrass me with the leer in her tone, it worked quite well. I was clearly not in shape for her teasing. With no roof to shingle or furnace to replace at my house, I chose not to seek work at Saukdale Metal Products this summer. Besides, Rosa had made it clear that my presence each day in the workplace would make our relationship too difficult to disguise. As a result, Teresa was right. I had not seen her or Toni or the other women from the factory since last summer. At the moment, I wished Teresa had not seen me.

"Rosa's working in the food tent," Teresa prodded in a singsong voice.

"Oh," I replied, "is Toni around, too?"

"Toni's going to dance," Teresa said, "but Rosa's the one that I bet wants to see you. Come on."

Teresa took hold of my arm and started to tug me out of my chair. I held back and she nearly tipped the chair over with me in it. That split second of panic before righting myself conjured up a totally unexpected image, straight from the old western movies, of Mexican villages populated by quiet peasant women with shy smiles. Where were those women now? Teresa had to be the brassiest Mexican woman I ever knew. I caught myself in the stereotype and quickly amended my thought. What the hell, Teresa had to be the brassiest woman I ever knew, period.

"Easy, easy," I said, "I don't want to tip over, thanks, and Rosa is probably way too busy to see me right now."

"Uh-oh, Teach is shy."

Teresa held her firm grip on my arm, and I followed in her wake toward the food tent.

"Hey, Rosa, look who's here," Teresa announced loudly as she pulled me into the tent and back to the tables where several women were hard at work.

"Hi, Teach." Rosa feigned surprise.

Her act appeared to fool Teresa, a task made fairly simple by someone so absorbed in her own antics.

"Got you working, I guess," I said, playing along with the little charade.

"That's life," Rosa answered. "Put handles on dustpans during the week, then spread beans on tortillas for the weekend."

"I'll bet you're good at it," I kidded.

"Sure," Rosa said as she rolled her eyes slightly.

"Actually, everything was really good," I said. "I'm glad I came."

Teresa had wandered off in search of some new adventure, but I noticed an older Mexican woman with streaks of gray in her jet black hair edging closer to us. She shot a glance in my direction as Rosa turned to talk to her.

"*Mira mami, el trabajo con nosotros en la factoria verano pasado.*"

The older woman looked at me with a worn face showing deep creases around her eyes and mouth. She nodded with a friendly smile.

"This is my mother," Rosa said.

I smiled back and gave an awkward, half-wave of my hand, not knowing what else to do.

"The dancing will start soon, Teach," Rosa said as a broad hint for me to exit the kitchen area that I felt sure no other man had invaded all day.

"Oh yeah, I want to watch that. Nice to see you, Rosa."

I left the tent wishing that she would be one of the dancers, but I knew that would not be the case. She told me more than a month ago that the young and pretty girls made up the dance group for the Mexican Fiesta. Now, I could see a line of almost two dozen young women forming in the open space at the front of the fiesta courtyard. I recognized Toni Martinez standing very near the center of the group. Each of the dancers wore a white blouse and black skirt, both pieces decorated with brightly-colored embroidery. To my eye, I saw no face as pretty or as gentle as Rosa's. Even so, I heard in their voices and watched in their steps a lightness I rarely saw in her. She was older, not so much by the calendar as by the hint of melancholy that too often closed around her like a fine, gossamer mist.

I looked back at Rosa still working in the food tent then turned my attention to the dancers as the music started. The courtyard came to life in song and step, but a heavier mist of my own sadness began to close around me. I moved unnoticed along the edge of the crowd, caught Rosa's eye with a slight nod and smile, and headed toward my car parked at the bottom of the hill.

October 18, 1975

Rosa loved to snuggle, and today both of us felt in a particularly snuggly mood. Our drive through the countryside had wound along all the back roads I knew that criss-crossed the Plum River. The rolling hills and gentle knolls formed by the river valley wore a subtle coat of autumn colors with brown oaks and faded yellow willows highlighted by small dashes of red sumacs and orange sugar maples. We had wandered much of the afternoon with no regard for time, stopping only once for sweet, caramel-covered taffy apples at Nelson's Orchard.

As we had on so many of our secret days of the past two years, Rosa and I ended our meanderings at the Town's Edge Motel. The owner assigned us room six as he had many times before. I took this not as a coincidence but as the gentleman's message that he knew the truth about Mr. and Mrs. Tim Johnson of Brenton, Illinois. His now friendly smile removed any concern one way or the other; and a Friday night movie, a trip to the new shopping mall in the cities, or just a drive in the country usually ended at the Town's Edge.

"It was fun today," Rosa whispered, curling up even closer to me.

"Mm, I know. The air gets so clear at this time of year. It's almost like a surprise every fall to see the color so crisp on a day like today."

"Do you ever think about writing things down?" she asked out of the blue.

"What do you mean?"

"You're smart, T. Sometimes, you say things you've seen, and I've never really seen it until you say it. I'll bet with your education and everything, you could write about it."

"I had a friend who used to write poetry," I said, "but I don't think I'm a writer."

"I still bet you'd be good at it, T."

"How about my turn for a question?" I asked. "Why don't you ever call me Jim?"

"T is your nickname. I think it's cute. You don't like it?"

Rosa had shortened Teach to T early on in our relationship, and I did like it, particularly with her soft Mexican accent. Still, something in me really longed to hear her call me Jim, if only once in a while.

"I like it fine. It's just that you never call me Jim . . . I mean even when we're close."

"You're serious, aren't you?" Rosa said softly.

"Um, sort of. I'm not that upset, exactly. I think I would just like it once in a while."

"Can I tell you the truth?" Rosa paused. "I'm . . . it won't sound right, but I'm afraid. See, I can call you T and not lose control, not fall too far in love with someone named T. If I call you Jim, that's too real. It's not safe for me to call you Jim. I could fall too far in love with someone named Jim."

"Would that be so bad?"

"Not bad, T . . . hard. It would be too hard. My family is from a different world. You're not part of that world, and I'm not part of yours."

"When we're together, you are my world, Rosa. I could meet your family."

"How should I introduce you? Maybe I can tell them, 'Here is the man I sneak away with to screw.'"

"Oh come on, be reasonable for a minute!" I snapped.

"You be reasonable, T. When I go home, we speak in Spanish. How much Spanish have you learned in two years?"

"I'm just saying we could try."

"Try what?" she said. "You're not Mexican, you're not Catholic, you're not anything my family wants."

"But what do you want, Rosa?" I asked with my voice softening.

She reached up and gently touched her small hands to my cheeks.

"Right now, I want a kiss," she whispered, pressing her lips against mine. She slowly pulled away and whispered again, "What I don't want is to have a guy come home at night and expect me to make him a tuna noodle casserole."

I saw the teasing glint in her eyes and answered, "Well, I don't want some woman to feed me refried beans every night."

"And I don't want those little white doilies on the backs of all my furniture," she said.

"I for sure don't want velvet pictures of horses or Elvis all over the house," I countered.

"I'm not spending all my money on funny hats with pink flowers to wear to church on Sunday," Rosa laughed.

"I suppose you want me to spend all my money on grease to slick back my hair."

"Oh, T, that was mean," she said. "You were too mean."

"And you are too sweet. As sweet as those nice, round taffy apples we had at Nelson's." I lightly patted her behind.

"Okay," she answered, poking her finger in my ribs, "but just remember it's the nice round apples people like, not the skinny, white wooden sticks that hold them."

I started to laugh at her tickling, and Rosa broke into a laugh of her own. Our laughter grew harder and harder until the bed in room six at the Town's Edge Motel began to shake for the second time that afternoon.

September 18, 1976

"Take a look around, Jim. There must be two hundred people already, and the sale doesn't start for another thirty minutes."

"Well, the auction bill lists a lot of antiques. You know that brings out the buyers these days," I said to Howard Miller.

"The nice weather helps, too. It's supposed to be seventy-eight and no rain in sight for three days," Howard said. "Still, I think curiosity brought fifty percent of 'em out here. People just want to see what Irene had stashed away in that house for the last forty years."

"You're probably right."

"I guess three full flatbeds and seven rows of furniture ought to make everybody happy. This has got to be twice as big as the last five or six auctions I've been to."

"Then, I hope you've got your money ready, Howard," I kidded.

Howard simply dismissed that notion with a wave of his arm as I moved to the other side of the flatbed trailer we were leaning against. Boyer Brothers Auctioneers out of Spenceville had asked me to work the sale as a helper today. The attorney for Irene Mitchell's estate hired Boyer Brothers because they ran the biggest auction service in the area. Even so, they needed extra help for a sale this size.

I began my day earlier in the morning setting out the cardboard boxes filled with miscellaneous goods that occupied the three flatbeds. Now, I drifted among the crowd, watching that no one shifted items from box to box. A good auctioneer knew how to move a lot of junk by putting it in a box with one or two good items, but the profit could go out the window if a couple of shrewd buyers shuffled things around at the last minute. I patrolled the flatbeds with a watchful eye to discourage any creative rearranging.

Over the past few years, I had gained a reputation as someone who could help out preparing for an auction or assisting the clerk. The occasional job for a local auctioneer could provide a Saturday or Sunday afternoon diversion without ever growing into a larger commitment than I wanted. I controlled the commitment, in part, by working only for auctioneers that I liked. Neither Harold nor Fred Boyer fit into that category.

Harold and Fred built Boyer Brothers from scratch into the biggest auction service in a four-county area. Unfortunately, they never tired of recounting the story of their rise from humble beginnings to auction moguls. Most other auctioneers privately called Harold and Fred "the Bore You Brothers." This time, I gladly accepted their invitation to work the auction today. Today, I wanted to keep busy. More than any Saturday I could remember, I needed the diversion.

The two hundred fifty people gathered on the lawn of the Mitchell place made the auction one of the biggest happenings in West Fork all year. Still, for me, a much larger event would take place this morning in Saukdale. At eleven o'clock, Rosa Rios would walk down the aisle of Our Lady of Guadalupe Church and hold out her hand to Joe Hernandez. They would come back down that aisle together as husband and wife.

Joe had moved in next door to Rosa's family last fall. He came to Saukdale to work in his uncle's asphalt roofing company and took a room in his uncle's house. When Rosa's father broke his leg in January, Joe was next door. I heard in January how helpful he was. I heard in February what a good man he was. In March, I heard what I didn't want to hear: Rosa had accepted a date with Joe. At twenty-four, Rosa needed to find a Catholic, a Mexican, and a good man. I needed to step aside. I did.

"Say, Jim."

Ed Johnson's voice roused me from my thoughts.

"Yeah, Ed."

"What time do you think they'll sell the car?" he asked.

"You mean the Dart?" I shot back with a smile.

Ed smiled, too. Irene Mitchell drove a Dodge Dart back and forth to work in Spenceville each day until she retired three years ago. Every evening, she pulled it into a bay in the large, three-car garage on the back of her lot and parked it right next to her father's 1948 Fraser. The Fraser had been Dr. Mitchell's last car, and everybody in West Fork knew it sat in nearly mint condition in the old garage. A man who loved machines as much as Ed Johnson had to be interested in the Fraser.

"You know which car I mean."

"Well, Ed, the flatbeds go first and that should take two hours, anyway, with all this stuff piled up. Then, I know the appliances and junk furniture will come next. It's just a question of whether they save the cars or the antiques for last. Either way, those cars aren't selling before one o'clock."

"You pretty sure?" Ed prodded. "I don't usually close the welding shop until noon on Saturdays, but I want to be here when the Fraser sells."

"I wouldn't worry about it. You get back here by a quarter after twelve, and you'll have plenty of time for a barbecue and a piece of pie before they ever get to that car."

"Okay, thanks." Ed turned and headed back to his shop.

I surveyed the flatbeds once more and thought of old Charlie, the notorious box rearranger. Charlie died two summers ago. I suppose that made my job easier today, but I still missed him among the regular cast of characters.

The twins were here, of course, staking out the boxes of books on the far flatbed. The collection of books Dr. Mitchell and Irene had gathered over the years promised a potential bonanza to the twins if the big crowd didn't drive the bidding up too high. That worry showed clearly on the identical features of the two women, and their faces appeared even more strained and taut than usual.

As Fred Boyer opened the bidding atop the first flatbed, I took a position perched on the wagon tongue to help identify bidders' numbers and still be available to run sheets to the clerk's table. The pace of the auction seemed to move more slowly than usual as box after box came up for sale; and by the second flatbed, my mind drifted more and more frequently to Saukdale and Our Lady of Guadalupe Church. Harold Boyer must have sensed flagging interest in the rest of the crowd, as well, and adopted an impromptu change in strategy as the last box left the second flatbed.

"Now, folks, we've got a big crowd here, today," Harold shouted from the edge of the empty wagon. "We want to give everybody a good chance to see all the merchandise without too much crowding. I'm gonna have our crew bring up some of these smaller furniture items and we'll sell 'em right off the trailer here. You can all get a good look, and we can open some space in the yard around the bigger pieces. We've got a lot of real nice items here, and I don't want anybody to miss anything."

I could see the twins' faces sink at the prospect of waiting even longer to get to the books on the final flatbed, but I took the cue from Harold Boyer and picked up a small wicker clothes hamper to carry over to the trailer.

"Okay, folks, here we go. What have we got here?" Harold cried.

"A nice-looking clothes hamper," Fred answered.

"Well, I guess it is. Why I believe I'd go out and get my clothes dirty just to put something in a hamper this nice," Harold shouted. "What are my bids? I'll take ten dollars. Do I have five? Five? Well then, two and go. Two dollars."

"Yes!" Fred yelled, pointing to the back of the crowd, and the bidding began again.

Steadily, we worked our way down the first row of furniture, pulling out any item light enough to lift up easily onto the flatbed wagon. With each piece, we moved closer to the one item I knew I wanted. Mixed in among all of Irene's possessions were a handful of things she had used to furnish the little house I rented from her when I first came to West Fork. Near the end of this row of furniture stood a small, three-shelf bookcase that once held the handful of books I brought with me as a new teacher.

The mahogany-stained, Stick-style bookcase was a nice little antique, but it meant much more to me than its modest monetary value as a collectible. In December of 1969, the top shelf of that bookcase became the setting for my Christmas village. Linda gave me the village, a tiny set of simple carvings from Czechoslovakia. She bought the set in Laurel and gave it to me on Christmas Eve just before we each headed to our respective parents' homes for the holiday. The houses, about the size of Monopoly game pieces, had spots and dashes of brown and red paint to depict stone walls and tile roofs. Plain turnings with green knobs on top represented trees, and little blocks carved into horses and men populated the streets of the Christmas village. It occupied the same bookcase each year until I bought my house.

Though Linda and I could never again share the joy of setting out the Christmas village, I wanted to place it once more on that simple top shelf where she had seen it last. I handed the bookcase up to Fred Boyer and waited for the bidding to start.

"Folks, you must have a niche at home that could use a bookcase like this," Harold exclaimed.

"It's a sturdy one." Fred tapped the top shelf for emphasis.

"All right, how about thirty-five dollars for the bookcase?" Harold shouted.

I waited for the auctioneer to drop the opening bid down, but I heard Fred Boyer yell out an immediate "Yes!"

"Thirty-five it is! Do I hear forty? Let's hear forty, forty."

"Yes!" called Fred's voice as I raised my hand.

"I got forty, now forty-five. I got forty, forty-five."

"Fifty!" came a bid from off to my left.

I turned my head, knowing already that I would see Vern from Vern's Antiques. I had witnessed this performance before. With a large crowd on hand, Vern figured the best way to come up with any later bargains for himself was to scare off as many casual buyers as possible. He would bid up the first antique item or two faster and further than he wanted to pay, leaving the impression that he would not be beaten and rival bidders would pay dearly for any antiques that day.

"I've got fifty, give me sixty," Harold shouted, shifting gears as auctioneers often did when sensing a spirited fight.

I raised my hand again and the "yes" rang out over the crowd. Vern went seventy as I figured he would, and I prepared myself to spend much more for this bookcase than I would earn for my labors at the auction today.

"Seventy-five!" I yelled before Harold could break into his pitch again. I could feel Vern's glare as he answered with eighty, and I watched Harold smile as I snapped back eighty-five.

"Eighty-five, ninety. Eighty-five, ninety. Will you go ninety?" Harold asked, sensing the end of the battle. "Eighty-five once, eighty-five twice. Sold to Jim Blair for eighty-five dollars. I'll tell you what, folks, he wanted that bookcase so bad, I'm gonna have to sell him some of those books in a few minutes."

The crowd laughed at Harold Boyer's banter. I only smiled—a warm, deep, satisfied smile.

December 15, 1980

I recognized the writing immediately and opened the Christmas card from Rosa before I even stepped out of the post office. While Rosa still lived in Sauk-dale, I had seen her only from a distance on a couple of occasions when I was downtown shopping. Now that she and Joe had moved to Iowa, she could just as well have been a million miles away. Joe took Rosa and their two boys to Iowa just before Christmas last year. He thought a cousin could help him get work in a tire factory.

I figured this card would have news of the new job. That was okay as long as they were her words—words that I could play through my mind and hear the soft accent of Rosa's voice. On our last day together, I asked her not to disappear completely from my life. She promised to send a Christmas card, and I told her I only needed to know that she was well and happy. She kept her promise, and now, I quickly scanned my fourth Christmas card from Rosa.

> Dear T,
> I hope you are fine as you read this note. I always remember you and hope you do not forget me.
> This year went by so fast but not so easy. Joe couldn't get on at the factory like he wanted so he went to roofing. Things

got pretty tight and I couldn't work, what with the baby. That's right. I'm a mama again. Carlos Alberto Hernandez. He was born on October 3, 1980 and we named him after my father. Maybe that's why the year went so fast, because the boys grow so fast. It seems like Carlos, Ramon, and little Joe need clothes or shoes or something everyday. I shouldn't complain. At least they are well and so are me and Joe.

I hope 1981 is a good year for you.

Always,

Rosa

I brushed away the flakes of snow that had fallen on Rosa's note and tucked the card back into its envelope as I walked toward the West Fork Store.

The snow floated down in big fluffy flakes, the kind of snowfall that rarely lasted long but let the world see the distinctive, lacy pattern of each individual snowflake. I had the feeling that a long-past winter day like this first gave somebody the idea that no two snowflakes are alike. I always wondered about this bit of scientific knowledge. Out of the trillions of snowflakes in Siberia or Alaska or Antarctica, I had a feeling that maybe, just maybe, several hundred absolutely identical ones might be found lying around if only there were a way to look. No matter, I had told my third graders on Friday that no two snowflakes are ever alike.

Snowflakes were our class art project for Christmas. I didn't always know what to do with third graders, but they were mine. This fall, the Plum River, Sharon, and Spenceville districts merged to form the new South Prairie School District. Our school became the West Fork Attendance Center, K-3, and I got the third grade. At least third graders could use sharp scissors, and yesterday, I had twenty-one eight-year-olds furiously folding and cutting white typing paper into snowflakes. Luckily, no two came out alike: a clear case of art imitating life, or the other way around, I wasn't sure which. Either way, the kids enjoyed themselves. It did seem a pity that we would be out of school right before January first, because our Christmas project easily created enough confetti for a New Year's Eve celebration.

I walked into the store a good twenty minutes earlier than my customary Saturday morning appearance. Even so, Howard Miller and Wayne Mitton, two of the other Saturday stalwarts, were already there. Wayne and Howard had taken up positions next to a stepladder, superintending Bill Dublin's efforts to install a smoke detector. With Margaret nowhere to be seen, I poured myself a cup of coffee and sat down at the table with the morning's copy of the *Saukdale Leader*. I picked up the paper intending as usual to scan the headlines, then turn immediately to the sports section; but a story near the bottom of the front page short-circuited my normal pattern: "Anti-War Bomber's Sentence Reduced, Wilson Eligible for Immediate Parole."

No thought of Dean Wilson had entered my mind in years. During his trial and conviction for bombing the ag research lab at Michigan A&E, I mustered only a distant and dazed interest in the news stories. At that time, the fact that Linda and I had once spent a miserable Fourth of July with Dean and his girlfriend, Jan, held no meaning for me. When the bombing occurred, a tragedy on Lake Michigan swept away all my concern for any other news of that day, or many days to come. Now, unexpectedly, the front page of the *Saukdale Leader* brought back memories of Dean Wilson, Laurel, Michigan, and November 1970:

> The Justice Department announced today that the conviction of anti-Vietnam War activist Dean Wilson would be reduced to a lesser charge. A 1971 jury found Wilson guilty of two counts of second-degree murder in the bombing of an agriculture building at Michigan A&E University. Wilson's conviction will be reduced to involuntary manslaughter. The action makes Wilson eligible for immediate parole.
>
> Two Laurel, Michigan firefighters lost their lives in the November 1970 bombing and blaze. Information released today indicates that both died from inhaling toxic chemicals. The possibility of unsafe practices in the agricultural research laboratory consumed by the fire influenced the reduction of Wilson's sentence.
>
> During his trial, Wilson claimed he planted only a small percussion bomb in a cold air duct connecting to the lab. He testified that he intended to blow red chalk dust into the lab to protest the "bloody war."
>
> The lab was conducting research on a powerful defoliant for use in Southeast Asia. According to the Justice Department, "firefighters responding to the incident possibly caused the spill of a small volume of highly volatile and toxic chemicals."

Reached for comment about the tragedy, retired Laurel fire chief, Albert Jensen, confirmed that his department responded to a "small fire at the lab." According to Jensen, he "pulled everybody back when my two men went down and just tried to contain the fire." The building sustained extensive damage in the blaze.

In Washington, Defense Department officials offered no comment on the decision to reduce Wilson's conviction. They did confirm that all research on the chemical defoliant ceased shortly after the fire.

The warden at the federal prison where Wilson is confined commented that "he has been a model prisoner (and) probably the most important person in our prison literacy program. He has helped a lot of other inmates." Wilson's attorney said that he hopes to continue work with literacy if he receives parole.

The time Wilson has already served qualifies him for an immediate parole hearing.

"That's a bag of bullshit," a voice behind me said.

I glanced up to see Bill Dublin looking over my shoulder. He and Howard slid into chairs at the table, while Wayne Mitton picked up a donut to go with his coffee.

"I can't believe that Wilson guy can get out of prison," Bill continued.

"I saw that at seven o'clock this morning," Howard said. "The guy kills two firemen, and he serves eight years in prison. I say they should change his sentence. They should make it twice as long."

"I don't know, Howard," I said. "How responsible was he if the government was messing with chemicals that dangerous?"

"How responsible? I'll be the first one to say how responsible," Howard answered with his voice rising. "One hundred and ten percent responsible. One guy started the fire and he was that one guy. Two guys died, and if you ask me, that makes it life in prison times two."

"Well . . ." I started.

"Would you look at this," Wayne interrupted. He gave a low whistle. "Look at what that Wyatt kid did last night."

Wayne never interrupted anyone, but now, he tossed the sports page from the newspaper down in the center of the table and whistled again for emphasis. The bold headline across the top of the page read, "CIU Upsets Loyola; Wyatt Scores 31."

"Wow," I said. "That's a heck of a game."

"I knew when that kid went to Central he would make it big," Bill Dublin said. "He was the best high school basketball player who ever came out of this whole area."

"What is he?" Wayne asked. "A senior now?"

"Nope, he's just a third-year man," Howard answered as his anger about Dean Wilson quickly dissolved in his well-known enthusiasm for basketball. "I'll bet he averages twenty-five points a game this year. He could even make second or third team All-American."

I never knew anyone who liked talking about basketball more than Howard Miller. I had a feeling the fact that it could be described with so many statistics made the game dear to his heart. I braced myself for a torrent of numbers about Calvin Wyatt's performance last year, but Bill spoke first.

"Hey, Jim, didn't your kids beat Calvin Wyatt's team in the junior high tournament one year?"

"No," I answered, "we won the tournament in '72, but we played Saukdale Fairwoods in the championship game. They actually beat Wyatt's team in the semifinals."

"They must have been pretty good, too." Bill said.

"Darn right," Wayne agreed.

"One thing's for sure, they were tall for eighth graders," I said.

"You can say that again," Howard said. "They had three kids over six-feet tall. You know, all three of those kids and one of their two starting guards are playing small-college ball now—four different teams, too."

"How'd you beat that bunch?" Wayne asked.

"Coaching!" I fired back to laughs all around the table. "No, we had Billy Kimball. I'll tell you what, he could do anything on a basketball court. Then, the other kids just pitched in and did their part. They were all good kids. You know, Tom Conley, Chuck Peterson, Ronnie Harper, Craig Jensen, CJ Martin."

"Darn right."

"I'll tell you, though," I said, "we couldn't have beaten Calvin Wyatt's team. He was just too much of an athlete, and he was even bigger than any of those Fairwoods kids. You know, I never saw so many really big eighth graders as there were that one year."

"Seems like Saukdale would've made it to state when those kids were all in high school," Bill said.

"They got beat three times in the sectional championship," Howard answered. "Three years in a row by less than five points each time. Each year, it was a different team from the cities. The last year, they lost by one point. One point!"

"That should've been their year," I said.

"Kinda shows just how much your team did winnin' the junior high tournament," Bill said.

"Coaching," I joked again.

"I'm gonna miss having a West Fork team," Howard said. "I went to all sixteen games every year for nine years."

"Well, this consolidation was bound to happen," I said. "We just don't have the same number of kids anymore."

"It was still nice having our own school." Bill shook his head. "And those games were good times for a lot of people, not just the kids."

"They were," I agreed.

"Darn right," Wayne Mitton added.

April 2, 1984

The wind rattled the doors on the machine shed at Art Kimball's farm. I could still call it Art's farm. That would end in a couple of hours. Right now, I sat alone at the small clerk's table set up for the auction. At the end of the auction, this would no longer be Art Kimball's farm.

I had not clerked at an auction for almost three years. In fact, I even stopped going to sales when too many farms of too many friends became too much of the auction business. Today, I made an exception. Billy Kimball asked me to be here today, and I knew I couldn't turn Billy down. When I coached him in the fifth grade, Billy wanted to be a farmer. When we won the county junior high school basketball tournament, Billy wanted to be a farmer. As high school graduation approached, Billy wanted to be a farmer. Tomorrow, at age twenty-six, Billy would no longer be a farmer. Today, Billy needed his friends.

"Hey, Jim, how about a cup of coffee?" Art Kimball shouted over the wind as he walked into the metal shed.

"Thanks." I reached for the Styrofoam cup he held out. "It's a little raw, even in here, with that wind so strong."

"I know. It's pretty cold for this time of year. A sunny day would make it nicer," Art said. "Okay if I join you?"

"Sure, Art. Sit down."

"Quite a few people here, don't you think?"

"Yeah, it looks like a good crowd. Guys know you take good care of things. That should help the bidding."

"I appreciate you doing this, Jim."

"Oh, it's nothing. You know I'd help you and Billy any way I could."

"Well, I'm okay," Art said. "I don't like it, but I'm okay. Billy's taking it a lot harder. I just don't know how to . . ."

Art's voice trailed off, and we both stared out the open end of the machine shed. A large cluster of men in quilted vests and seed corn hats moved at intervals down a long row of machinery lined up in last year's soybean field. First, the small orange utility tractor sold, then the silvery, galvanized metal elevator. Gradually, the group migrated toward the large green and yellow combine the auctioneer had positioned to be the last piece of equipment up for sale.

"You know," Art spoke again, "he's out there watching every piece of machinery being sold. You never, Jim . . . when you have a son . . . I mean you never dream things can turn out this way."

"I know, Art," I answered, not really knowing at all, but knowing only by his rambling words that Art wasn't any more okay than Billy.

"Look, I didn't mean to go on. I've got things set up to work out. Just not on the farm."

"I know you'll come out of it, Art. Have you got plans?"

"Yeah, I've got a job lined up in Saukdale, and I'm getting us out of the farm while there's still something left."

"That's good, at least," I said.

"That's what I told Billy, but he doesn't want to accept it. You know, for the last few years farmers had to get bigger or die. We just got bigger at the wrong time. Right when we bought our last land, the interest just went through the roof; but with the money out on the land, we still had to borrow to put in crops and buy equipment. The interest ate us up. We've lost money three years in a row. I just don't want to borrow any more. We get out now and there's still equity in the farm. It's not everything we put into it, but it's still something. Something for June and me. Something for Billy, too. We wait any longer and I don't know."

"What's the new job?" I asked in hope of a brighter subject.

"Oh, I've got a friend in Saukdale with a small engine shop. You know, lawn mowers, snowmobiles, outboards, that sort of thing. He knows I'm handy, and he can't keep up with all the work he's got."

"Sounds good," I said.

"Well, it doesn't pay much, but we don't need that much. June and I will stay right here in the house. We'll keep the outbuildings. The land will sell, but nobody needs another barn. Half the farms around here don't have stock anymore, anyway. They don't need their own barns. Ralph, the guy I'm working for, he figures I can pick up quite a bit of cash renting the barn and the machine shed for boat storage. He's got several customers looking for places to keep their boats over the winter. I guess there's not any money for farming these days, but there's plenty for buying boats."

"I don't know, Art. It seems that way," I said. "How about Billy? Does he have any plans?"

"Nothing for sure," Art sighed. "He says he'd like to move up to Wisconsin where we go fishing. There's some construction work up there. He's talked about driving a truck."

"You don't think he'll stay around here?"

"No. I wish it could be like that, but there's too many memories," Art answered in a raspy voice. "Billy should still be living with dreams. He's too young to be living just with memories."

I nodded my head. Art Kimball and I sat in silence and sipped our coffee.

April 10, 1988

   The crowd of people in the West Fork Store was beginning to dwindle as I sat and pondered the banner that read "Best Wishes Margaret." Doc had picked it up at the card shop in Saukdale. Apparently, making flimsy, plastic banners was something card shops could do now. I wondered when that happened. Last year? Five years ago?

   I suppose I could have asked the same question about the vinyl kitchen chair I was sitting in. It probably wasn't in the store when I came to West Fork. There had been kitchen chairs sitting here, to be sure, but it seemed like Bill and Margaret were always replenishing the stock. As a back loosened or a seat tore on one chair, another old castoff took its place. When did this one appear? Last year? Five years ago? But now, there would be no more replacement chairs. Bill passed away three months ago, and Margaret had decided to close the store.

   There also would be no more Saturday morning coffee. Three weeks ago, the regulars in the coffee crew decided we should do something for Margaret. Then, we weren't sure what to call it. Retirement party didn't seem right. None of us actually knew whether or not Margaret would need to find some type of job. Farewell party sounded too final, although Margaret was moving to Missouri to be closer to her children. Besides, how could we use the word *party* at all with Bill's death so near and so much of the reason why there would be no West Fork Store?

We settled on open house, an open house at the store. Holding the whole thing in the basement of the Methodist Church probably would have made more sense. As it was, Arlene Mitton had to borrow the 100-cup coffeemaker from there, anyway. Thank God most of our Saturday morning crew had wives. Who knows what we would have come up with on our own, but the women had covered card tables with paper tablecloths and filled them with ham sandwiches on buttered hamburger buns, bowls of potato salad, sweet pickles, mixed nuts, and paper party plates. Even with the store shelves half-empty, it looked like a party.

On a table in front of the cash register, a large sheet cake decorated with blue and white frosting also read "Best Wishes Margaret." A backup sheet cake rested on the checkout counter. As Arlene had told us, "The cake doesn't always go, but you can't take a chance on running out."

Doc figured that much cake had to produce a thirst for milk, and I volunteered to bring three gallons. This morning, I had placed them in one of the store's empty coolers. There hadn't been a store-closing sale. Margaret just stopped ordering. The perishables were gone ten days ago. She found a store liquidator who would take what was left of the rest, even the canned goods and boxes of instant pudding. This morning, I brought three gallons of milk to the store where I had purchased more quarts than I could count in the past twenty years.

"A penny for your thoughts."

I glanced to my right, though that wasn't necessary to identify the speaker. Margaret Dublin and my mother, before she died, were the two people who could use all the common phrases and clichés and never have them sound old or tired.

"I'm not sure they're worth a penny."

"I guess I'm losing my business sense. Probably a good thing that I'm closing this place up."

I searched for a witty reply—and came up empty.

"Never mind about that," Margaret said. "I came looking for you. I've got something in the back. I thought maybe you'd want it."

I followed Margaret into the living quarters in the back of the store. I realized that I had been in Bill and Margaret's living room only two or three times in twenty years. It seemed that between trips to the store, church bazaars, Fourth of July picnics, school graduations, and picking up the mail, among dozens of public encounters, people in West Fork were practically tripping over each other every day. There wasn't much need to invite your neighbors into your home.

"You wait here," Margaret said. "I've been going through things, and the rest of the house is a mess."

I glanced around the room. It was just as I remembered. Lived in, but neat, and still dominated by Bill's leather recliner and 33-inch television set.

"Have a seat," Margaret yelled from upstairs. "I'll be right back down."

"I'm okay," I shouted back.

I heard Margaret's footsteps returning down the stairs and saw a small snapshot in her hand as she came into the room.

"I found this last night," she said, holding it up to me. "That's Will."

In the center of the picture, a teenage boy stood holding a cardboard box with one side cut out. Whatever was in the box was too small to make out clearly but looked more like doll furniture than anything else.

"Will must have been in college when you came to town. Probably grad school, since Ann must have been in college by then, too."

"Yeah," I answered.

I knew the names of Bill and Margaret's children as well as I knew those of the people who lived in West Fork, but both had been grown, married, and moved away for years. I had met Ann once or twice, but Will must have come back only at Thanksgiving or Christmas when I was at my parents' home.

"Will was some kind of officer in the Junior Red Cross. This was when he was a freshman in high school. They had an assembly, and he gave a report about building a fallout shelter in your house."

"Okay."

"Not making any sense, am I?" Margaret said. "They brought in the kids from the country schools. Linda Bray was a school captain or whatever Junior Red Cross called them. I think they were the ones who were supposed to tell the other kids to get under the desks in case of an atom bomb."

I looked closely at the background of the picture and saw a young Linda, pre-contact lens days, with glasses that came to a point on each side like the fins on a '57 Chevrolet. She was seated on stage in a row of chairs with other kids her age, probably the captains from the rest of the country schools. She was mostly bony shoulders, sharp elbows, knobby knees, and skinny arms and legs, but I could see in the serious, determined look on her face, the young woman she would blossom into—the Linda I would meet only a few years later.

"Imagine," Margaret said. "Telling little kids to jump under their desks. As if the Russians were going to bomb Ed Johnson's welding shop or anybody could get under those country school desks, anyway, the way they were all bolted together.

141

We probably scared them all to death."

Or made them question war, I thought to myself.

"Anyway, enough about that. The picture is yours, Jim, if you'd enjoy having it."

"I'd like that." In that moment, I realized that I had never seen pictures of Linda as a kid. For whatever reason, we never found the time to look at old pictures. Or maybe our time just ran out too soon.

"It's yours," Margaret said.

"But don't you want it, you know, with Will in it?"

"Oh, I've got lots. Bill was driving bus for the high school even then. He took the country school kids down to the assembly. Took his camera, too. He was always so proud of Will. Will and Ann, both."

"I know he sure talked a lot about both of them."

"Will was Bill, Jr., of course. I'm not sure now if it's a good idea to name a child after a parent. I probably should have thought more about that back then. Will never wanted to be Bill, Jr. or little Bill or Billy. That's where Will came from."

"I can understand that."

"I suppose now, Dr. William Dublin, Jr. makes a pretty impressive name for a professor." Margaret smiled and nudged me. "I think he gets a little full of himself sometimes."

"He's accomplished a lot," I said.

"His father did, too."

"Oh, I know, with the Navy and the store and . . . everything."

"You're one of the ones that's wondering, too, aren't you, Jim?"

"Wondering?"

"Wondering the same as the others," she said. "Why is Margaret packing up and leaving?"

"No, I think I understand."

"But it's too soon. Wait a year before you make any big decisions."

"I guess it seems a little soon."

"I would have done this the day after Bill died, if it hadn't been winter. Ann and her family are in Kansas City, and Will teaches at the university in Columbia. That's only a couple of hours apart."

"I suppose it's that you've always been here," I said. "When I think of you, I think of the store."

"Jim, there isn't any always. Even with Bill alive, it was just a matter of time for the store. The money it brings in has been going down for ten years."

Margaret reached out and patted my arm.

"Bill and I were married for forty-four years, but here I am. It wasn't forever. Here's what I learned. Whoever you care about, hold 'em close. You can figure out the rest of it later. I've got two kids and their families in Missouri. I'm going to Missouri."

We stood silently for a moment and then I asked, "Have you figured out any of the rest of it, what you'll do in Columbia?"

"Don't tell me you're gonna be like Howard and the rest of that bunch, figuring that I could find plenty to do in West Fork but nothing in Columbia with the whole big University of Missouri there."

"Maybe *I've* lived here too long," I said.

We both laughed, then hugged, then turned to walk to the front of the West Fork Store.

December 11, 1989

A faint, ironic smile formed on my lips as I sat in the outer office of Attorney Charles Sommers. The Saukdale Office Park occupied land where the Town's Edge Motel once stood, and Attorney Sommers' suite had to be within feet of, if not directly atop, the location of the old motel's room number six. So close to that special spot, I held this year's Christmas card from Rosa in my hands.

I grabbed my mail quickly after school this afternoon, afraid that I would be late for my appointment with the lawyer. I arrived right on time, only to learn that Attorney Sommers was running late, himself. I greeted that news from his secretary with feigned disappointment and inwardly celebrated my good fortune. I could open Rosa's card without delay.

> Dear Jim,
>
> It seems every year goes by a little bit faster than the one before. So much time has passed that writing this card makes me wonder what you look like after all these years. Probably the same skinny guy.
>
> One thing for sure, I am not the same young girl. I know that just by watching the kids grow up so fast. All four of them are in school now and sometimes I think little Joe

144

should still be a baby.

Joe's job at the highway department is going good. He just passed the test for supervisor, so we've got our fingers crossed that something will open up.

I still work at the college. The schedule works out real good. They don't want me to start in on the dorm until about ten o'clock when the students are mostly in class. I finish cleaning by two and get home before my kids are out of school. I work straight through lunch. That way I get done when I want. Also a good way to not get so fat!

I hope you are well and happy.

Bye for now,

Rosa

I shook my head and smiled again at Rosa's words. It had been many years, so many in fact, that Rosa felt safe calling me Jim. The first time I read Jim, instead of T, on her card, I felt a kind of hollowness deep in my chest; but now it produced only a wistful feeling. For an instant, some memory of a life that never happened would flash through my mind and I was somehow with Rosa. Yet with each passing year, that moment when dreams and memories blurred together grew shorter and shorter. Rosa could call me Jim now without letting herself care too much, and I could be happy for the life she had built without having to make myself care too little.

"Mr. Blair," the receptionist said, calling me back from my thoughts of Rosa, "Attorney Sommers can see you now. Go right in."

She pointed toward the door to my left, and I entered the lawyer's private office. Dark wooden bookcases covered most of three walls and ran nearly from floor to ceiling. Light filtered through the translucent cloth of the inner pair of a set of double drapes. They covered the large expanse of glass that constituted the greater portion of the fourth wall of the office. I could see through the fine mesh material that Attorney Sommers' office looked out into a courtyard, but the formal manner of the man motioning me to a chair suggested that he rarely, if ever, opened the inner drapes for a completely unobstructed view.

Attorney Sommers must have been in his late sixties, and I guessed that he had spent most of his legal career in a downtown office with a second floor location that admitted no possibility of a passerby gazing in his window. In the one-story Saukdale Office Park, he invoked the decorum of attorney/client confidentiality with a layer of translucent white cloth.

"Hello, Mr. Blair. Please sit down."

I seated myself in one of two wooden captain's chairs with dark leather upholstery. The lawyer sat on the opposite side of the large mahogany desk that dominated the office.

"Thank you, Mr. Sommers," I said as I sat down.

"Of course, you know why you are here, Mr. Blair."

"Yes, I understand it has to do with Helen Bray's will."

"That is correct," the attorney stated. "I have handled Helen's legal matters for many years. Actually, I was the family attorney when Mr. Bray, uh, was still alive."

Attorney Sommers stumbled over the last sentence. His hesitation seemed uncharacteristic for this formal man of the law, but some things never lose their power to stop words short no matter how many years pass. A suicide, particularly of a man like Don Bray, holds such power.

"At any rate," the lawyer continued, "you are here as a beneficiary in Helen's will."

"I have to say I was surprised by your call. Except for a Christmas card once a year, I never had any contact with Mrs. Bray after she moved."

"Actually, you are mentioned in the will in two distinct regards. I have a copy here for you to read carefully, but I believe it would be best, with your permission, if I summarize the will's contents for you."

"Please do."

"By the terms of Helen's will you are to receive ten thousand dollars. After this sum is paid to you and all of the bills and obligations for Helen's burial and other expenses of the estate are paid, the remaining proceeds will be equally divided two ways. Half of the money will go to Helen's one surviving sister. Helen provided for the other half of the money to be placed in trust to fund scholarships for students to attend college. Her will directs that this trust be named the James Blair Scholarship Fund."

"I beg your pardon?" I stammered in response to this surprise pronouncement from Attorney Sommers.

"Helen's will establishes a scholarship fund named after you, Mr. Blair. Obviously, I helped Helen prepare this will. She did not want you to have any knowledge of her plans until she passed away."

"I see, I guess."

"I believe if I continue, it will be fairly clear. Let me explain the trust to you," Attorney Sommers suggested. "Helen approached me about this idea several years ago. She told me at that time that she considered you a fine young man and a dedicated teacher. She wanted to recognize your dedication in this way. She had me draw up the trust to provide scholarships for students from the Plum River Elementary School District to attend college. Obviously, this was some time ago. The income generated by the trust is to be distributed as directed by the decisions of a three-person board of trustees. The trust specifically states that scholarship recipients must be making normal progress toward a four-year college degree and must be residents of the area that formerly constituted the Plum River School District. When the Plum River district consolidated with Sharon and Spenceville, Helen asked me to clarify the terms of the trust to ensure that the scholarship money would be restricted to students who resided within the boundaries of the former Plum River district. I presume this is clear to you, Mr. Blair."

"Sure, I understand about that," I answered. "I was a teacher at Plum River Elementary before we consolidated into South Prairie. I still teach at the West Fork Attendance Center. I'm just a little surprised by all of this."

"I can understand your surprise, but there are additional provisions, which Helen requested, that I must explain to you. She directed that you, Mr. Franklin Shelby, and the current principal of the South Prairie High School be asked to serve as the initial trustees for the scholarship fund. I will contact Mr. Shelby and Principal Andrews about their service. You would, of course, know both men?"

"Doc Shelby and I have been friends ever since I came to West Fork. I know Mr. Andrews through the district."

"And you are willing to serve as a trustee?" the lawyer asked formally.

"Oh, of course . . . I mean, it's an honor . . ." I stammered again. "What I mean to say is that it would be an honor even if my name didn't have anything to do with it."

"It can be more than just an honor, Mr. Blair. The trust will be able to be of genuine financial assistance to worthy students. We must settle all transactions involving the estate before arriving at exact numbers, and that will take several months. Nonetheless, my preliminary look at Helen's assets suggest that the scholarship fund will have a corpus in excess of two hundred fifty thousand dollars."

"That's a lot of money," I said.

"In truth, I would have expected it to be more. Helen held the farm for several years and managed to sell when the price of farmland was at its absolute peak." Attorney Sommers stopped abruptly as if reminded that the details of Helen Bray's personal finances were, in fact, none of my business. "I will have some papers for you to sign, Mr. Blair, confirming your willingness to serve as a trustee; and, of course, I will arrange the payment of Helen's personal bequest to you. If you have no further questions, I have yet one more appointment for the afternoon."

I nodded and offered a simple "thank you" as I shook Attorney Sommers' outstretched hand.

June 22, 1995

I turned my red Ford Escort wagon left onto the highway and headed north toward Saukdale. Already, the West Fork Attendance Center looked different. School had been out only three weeks, but the weeds grew prominently out of the cracks in the sidewalk and the crevices around the brick building's foundation. Maybe this happened, unnoticed, every summer. Still, I didn't remember it, and a feeling inside me said that the weeds knew. Somehow, they could tell that school had closed its doors in West Fork for the last time three weeks ago. In the fall, all students in all grades from all schools in the South Prairie district would attend classes at the new campus halfway between Spenceville and Sharon.

The emptiness of the schoolyard echoed the open fields that lined the highway as I drove north. The fences that once accompanied travelers every mile of the way from West Fork to Saukdale had all but disappeared. No hogs or cows remained to be fenced in on the large cash grain farms that consumed the western Illinois landscape. Through the years, two, then three, then four farms became one—and eight, then six, then four farmers became two. Now, a traveler could drive miles without seeing a fence, a cow, a pig, or a person. The corn and soybean fields seemed to edge closer to the highway each year as if someday they would take back every inch of the land that once belonged to some distant cousins in the plant world when prairie grass, unbroken by fences or highways, stretched as far as the eye could see.

Linda Bray and I had driven this route every workday of my first summer in West Fork. My thoughts rolled back to those June days more than quarter of a century ago, and my mind remained in that time long past until I came to a halt at the four-way stop for the highway bypass around Saukdale. A short honk of the horn from the pickup truck across the intersection summoned my thoughts back from those warm memories of 1969. I glanced at the cab of the truck and received a smile and a wave from the driver. Ironically, the familiar face of Jeff Larson served simply to add another layer to my ponderings of the path from past to present. I waved back as he drove by on his way, I guessed, to see Doc Shelby.

Jeff had operated his own veterinary practice in Saukdale for close to ten years, but I could still see in his face the thirteen-year-old boy who led the Pledge of Allegiance for the West Fork Veterans' Day dinner.

As I flashed back to that evening in the past, it symbolized how little we can know about the future. Who could have known that a young woman who stormed past me in a fury would become a part of my life, that her life's dream of becoming a veterinarian would never happen, that her father would briefly share the podium that evening with the eighth-grade boy who would live that dream instead. And surely, no one present that night would have guessed that the sturdy, new brick school built for the future would sit empty before two full generations of students could walk through its doors.

The thoughts of future and past carried me many miles beyond Saukdale before I let my mind turn toward the present and the purpose of my trip. Fittingly, this journey itself reconnected the past to the present. I still remembered Tom Conley as the steady, determined kid who helped the Plum River Rangers win an all-county basketball championship. Those same traits doubtless propelled Tom's career in education to the point of becoming the youngest school superintendent in the state of Wisconsin. Tom called me after he heard the West Fork Attendance Center would close. The northern section of his district had its own rural attendance center that needed a sixth-grade teacher. Tom chuckled as he told me he was hoping whoever they hired could also coach the fifth- and sixth-grade basketball team. I hesitated at Tom's invitation to apply for the job; but when he persisted, I reluctantly agreed to "come up to Wisconsin for just a look around."

I could tell over the phone that Tom wondered if my hesitation about the job somehow involved him. In actual fact, only my pride in his career and the location of his district in extreme western Wisconsin allowed me to consider the opening at all. There was no way for him to know that I had not been in Wisconsin since November 1970. After the ferry tragedy that took Linda away from me, I would not, could not, go back into the state I had enjoyed so much before. Even now, I wondered if all the miles from western Wisconsin to Lake Michigan and all the years from 1970 to the present would be enough separation to let me live in the state.

The route I had traveled today underscored that sense of ambivalence about the destination. Throughout the morning and early afternoon, I had zig-zagged north and then west, north and then west over the Illinois countryside until I came to the Mississippi River about fifty miles south of Wisconsin. I pulled out a road atlas and calculated a drive of two-and-a-half more hours to my destination by following the highway that snaked along the Illinois and Wisconsin side of the river. Continuing the trip on the west side of the Mississippi would delay my eventual entry into Wisconsin without adding many miles to the journey. I turned my car onto the high bridge and headed over the river into Iowa. Wisconsin could wait.

The northeastern corner of Iowa belied the stereotype of a state with flat, unchanging land. At first, the highway climbed over broad hills with long slopes and large flat fields on top. Within an hour's drive, the hills came closer and steeper, separated by tight valleys that shepherded small streams and rivers between the high ground. Gradually, I tracked the return of livestock and fences along my route. While unfenced grain fields covered the flat hilltops, the areas of steep hillsides and tight valleys gave way to the smaller fields and fenced-in pastures of dairy farms. The sight of working barns, the presence of herds of black-and-white cows drinking from streams, and even the smell of manure in the air lured me off the U.S. Highway and onto a smaller, winding state road. I would not meet with Tom Conley until tomorrow morning, anyway. Wisconsin could wait.

I had already driven through two small towns when I came to the sign that read "Ferrisburg Pop. 1500." My watch showed 2:30 and my internal clock signaled time for a break. While the world may work mighty changes all around, most people carry a few personal traditions with them for a lifetime. I still punctuated long driving trips with a stop for coffee and a sample of the fare from the ovens of a local bakery or restaurant. Ferrisburg offered no bakery, but the Coffee Cup Cafe specifically promised to fill half the bill and seemed a good prospect, as well, for a piece of apple or cherry pie with ice cream.

I guided my car into a diagonal parking slot directly in front of the restaurant. Flat, square panels of red-and-white metal siding covered the facade of the small business building. Large plate glass windows flanked either side of the recessed entry door. Arched lettering on both windows spelled out "Coffee Cup Cafe." The red-and-black plastic sign hanging in the center of the glass door read "Open - Come In." A second sign in the same material and resting on one window ledge pronounced "FOR SALE BY OWNER."

I entered the door and found the Coffee Cup Cafe completely empty. A long counter with round stools stretched across the width of the room. Green vinyl booths lined the front and side walls of the cafe's dining area. My daylong musings about the past left me in a mood for privacy. Although the restaurant had no other customers, I moved to a booth in the corner and took a seat with my back to the rest of the room. I had spotted pieces of cherry, peach, and apple pie stacked in the cylindrical glass display cases on the counter. Peach pie with vanilla ice cream sounded good. I didn't bother to reach for the menu on the edge of the table.

The bell hanging from the front door had announced my presence when I entered, and now I heard the waitress approaching behind me. I sat patiently, elbows on the table, chin propped against my hands. I turned to look up when an unexpected splash of water across the table and into my lap startled me to attention. My sudden surprise as the waitress spilled a full glass of water in my direction could not compare to the look of shock that gripped her face and penetrated into the deep black pupils that stared down at me.

The eyes were the same with only the addition of fine crow's feet at the corners to mark the passage of time. A few gray strands peeked out of the short brown hair that still turned under at the ends. Even the look of utter desperation could not mask the fine features I remembered. I stared back, frozen by the same shock that must have jolted the glass of water out of her hand. I could not even brush away the pool of liquid that dribbled over the edge of the table and onto my legs. Finally, I managed a single faint word that mustered only enough strength to emerge as a whisper.

"Linda," I gasped.

"Please, Jim, don't say anything," she pleaded.

I saw her move quickly away from the table to grab a rag from behind the counter. In the shock of the moment, I couldn't focus my eyes to follow her movements, but I heard the sound of a salt shaker tumble from the counter, dislodged in her hasty grab for the piece of cloth.

"What's going on, Cindy?" a woman's voice called out from the kitchen.

"I just spilled some water," Linda yelled back quickly.

"Do you need some help?" the voice responded.

"No!" Linda barked instantly then recovered some control. "It's just water. I'm okay."

She sprang frantically back to my table. She swiped at the water in a near panic, as if capturing the spill could also wipe away the shock flowing through our bodies.

"What . . . what," was all that would come out as I tried to speak.

"Jim, please don't talk. Please!" she pleaded again.

Either the profound depth of emotion in her voice or the stunned disbelief that crashed over me in thundering waves prevented me from saying anything. Suddenly, I saw the tears well up in her eyes and flow down her cheeks. I could neither describe my emotions nor imagine hers. In some unknowable reflex of everyday life, I grabbed a wad of napkins from the dispenser on the table and placed them in her hand. She dropped the soaked counter rag and held the paper napkins to her face, wiping at her eyes, and drawing a shaky breath. I began to speak again, but Linda held a finger to my lips. With so little force remaining in my being, it took only a single touch to still the words that I tried to form.

"I know you don't understand. I know you can't understand," she said in a hushed, trembling voice. "I'll tell you everything. Just not here. I can't tell you here."

"Cindy, you got an order, honey?" the woman from the kitchen called out.

"No, not yet," Linda shouted back.

"Well, I gotta close down the grill pretty quick. I gotta clean it before we close up, you know."

"Yeah, that's okay. This is just coffee," Linda answered.

I could see the tears about to overcome her again as she turned back toward me.

"Please, Jim. Please go. You can come to my apartment."

"No, now just wait," I started, but she interrupted quickly.

"I promise you. I get off work in twenty minutes. I live a block from here, above the drugstore. I'll go right there in twenty minutes."

I struggled still to form words or gain any composure in a world that, in an instant, had changed more radically than I could ever have conceived. At last, I simply looked at Linda and nodded my head.

"Here's the number." She jotted something on the back of her order pad.

"201 1/2 Mill Street. It's only a block up the street, above the drugstore. Just go up the stairs. My apartment door has the letter A on it. It's the only apartment in the building. Come up at five minutes after three, and I'll be there. I promise."

Linda took hold of my hand and coaxed me out of the booth. I could feel my face tighten with apprehension as we moved toward the door. She acknowledged my unspoken protest with a tighter squeeze of my hand. The bell rang as I stepped out the front door of the Coffee Cup Cafe.

I dropped into the front seat of my car and slowly realized the awkwardness that sitting there for the next twenty minutes would present. Across the street, a historical marker stood on a grassy strip next to the river. The parking area by the marker could offer the plausible appearance of a traveler pulled over for a rest. I backed out of my parking place on the street and drew into a spot near the marker.

I checked my watch then turned my eyes back to the restaurant door. I couldn't lose Linda again. I repeated the pattern of my eyes between watch and door with such frequency that time barely seemed to move at all. Finally, I tried to direct my attention to the cast bronze marker. I read the large, bold title "John Ferris' Mill." I could go no further before returning my eyes to the door across the street. I couldn't lose Linda again.

The glass in the cafe door caught the reflections of trees rustling in the wind and cars driving down the street. Each movement in the glass quickened my pulse and raised my hope that the door would open.

The clock in my dashboard reached 3:00, and not a soul had moved through the door. My mind raced with uncontrollable thoughts and fears. Maybe Linda had told me the wrong closing time. Maybe I should go back into the cafe. Maybe Linda had used a rear door. Maybe none of this was happening at all.

The door opened at 3:02.

Linda stepped quickly onto the sidewalk and turned to start up the block. She walked briskly, covering real estate as rapidly as I remembered, but the bouncy spring that had once announced a buoyant enthusiasm to the world no longer marked her step. She headed directly up the street, looking neither right nor left.

I watched her cross the street at the corner and kept sight of her as she moved along three-quarters of the length of the drugstore building. The neighboring block of business buildings obscured my view of the rear corner of the drugstore. As soon as she disappeared from sight, I started the Escort and made my way toward her destination. I turned left at the corner and caught a glimpse of the door at the rear of the drugstore closing. It must have been Linda. It had to be

Linda. I couldn't lose Linda again.

I parked my car just past the alley that divided the block in two, and half-ran, half-walked to the door. A long flight of stairs took me to a small landing. A dark, narrow hall led to the left. A plain, white apartment door stood directly in front of me. The metal nameplate on the door held a thin slip of paper that read "C. James." I knocked firmly and heard the sound of footsteps headed in my direction. The door squeaked slightly as it opened, and Linda and I stood face to face.

"Come in, Jim."

I followed her down a short hall that opened into a small living room. A round, bay window jutted out from the corner of the building, flooding the room with light and creating an illusion of greater space. Plants lined the perimeter of the bay. A long sofa in a simple modern design with bright flowered upholstery occupied the center of the room. Two high-backed, white wicker chairs with seat pads flanked the front windows. A large floral print on the pads echoed the sofa, and I noticed a small black-and-white cat curled up to enjoy the afternoon sun in the chair to the right. The periphery of my vision revealed an open kitchen area to the left of the spot where I stood.

"This is where I live," Linda said simply.

"God, I can't believe you're alive at all."

"Please sit down, Jim. I'm going to try to explain it, all of it."

I felt a deep anger begin to replace the shock in my body. I wanted to find the words to express the hurt that had started to burn from within, but the very depth of my feelings again held me speechless. I sat stiffly on the sofa and looked across as Linda sank deep into one of the wicker chairs with one leg tucked up underneath her.

"This is so hard. I don't know where to start."

"Start anywhere," I answered abruptly. "I don't know anything."

"I guess it starts with Dean Wilson. Do you remember he was a friend of mine from Laurel College?"

I silently nodded my head.

"You know he went to jail for the bombing at Michigan A&E?"

"Yeah," I nodded again.

"Well, I was in a group with Dean, a group opposed to the war."

Linda could see my face begin to draw into a perplexed look.

"You see. I didn't understand everything about the group, or maybe, just about Dean. That bombing took place on the day I was supposed to come home for Thanksgiving, the day you were supposed to meet me at the ferry."

My face flushed red hot as I remembered that day, but I held back the tears that wanted to form inside me.

"I heard about the bombing on the radio," Linda continued, "in a coffee shop. Right away, I knew I had trouble. I had a ticket for the ferry, but I never got on."

"But Linda, what do you mean trouble? What trouble?"

"It was our group. Dean kept telling our group that the Ag lab building had military research for Vietnam going on. The university told the public it was just ordinary herbicide research, but Dean knew that part of the building had tightly restricted access. We all knew that. Dean figured that the restricted area had military projects. Our group, we were mad. We wanted to find the truth. That's where I got involved."

"Involved in a bombing?" I blurted.

"No, not really. I mean, I guess, not completely. I didn't know anything about any kind of a bomb. The group just asked me to make a few diagrams from inside the building, things like doors nobody could go in and where vents were. Dean said we could get an idea of how big the lab was, how many different spaces were involved. The area used to be some kind of storage. Anyway, I made the diagrams. It seemed like one way to find something out, and I was one person who had to go into the building a lot. That's why when I heard about the bombing and the firemen who died, I had to find out what happened. I didn't care about the ferry; I had to make some phone calls."

She paused for a deep breath.

"That's when everything started to happen so fast. I tried Dean's apartment but nobody answered. The same thing happened with two other members of the group. It took my fourth call to reach anybody. The guy's name was Larry Herman. He told me he thought Dean and some of the others had already been picked up for questioning. He sounded really worried, just like me. Larry had friends on a commune, up where the Michigan orchards are. He said I could probably go there. Maybe get lost until I could see what was happening. I caught a bus and headed that way twenty minutes later."

"But didn't you call your parents?"

"There wasn't time. When I got to the bus station, the bus was almost ready to leave."

"But what did you think about the ferry?"

"I knew you would worry when I wasn't on it, but I figured if you called my parents . . ."

"Your parents! I did call your parents! How can you talk about being worried? The God damned ferry sank! That's more than being worried. The God damned ferry sank!"

"I didn't know. That's it. I didn't know. When I got off the bus, I managed to get a ride to the commune, but it didn't have a phone. I asked them about the bombing. Somebody told me they heard on the radio that Dean Wilson had already been arrested. I didn't know anything about the ferry. Nobody told me a ferry had sunk. I asked these friends of Larry's about the bombing. They had no way to know that any news about the ferry would mean anything to me."

"But I talked to your parents that night."

"Wait, please. Let me try to explain," Linda pleaded. "That's what I'm saying. The commune didn't have a phone. I had to go back to the nearest town. It was almost midnight before I called Mom and Dad. They told me about the ferry, but first they told me the FBI had already been to our farm. My folks thought I was on the ferry. That's what they told the FBI. Do you see?"

"What do you mean, do I see? I don't see anything. Nobody ever told me anything."

"My phone call shocked my folks. Mom cried when she heard my voice. She was just happy I was alive. But then she figured out right away that the FBI didn't know that. Dad told me to come home and he would phone the authorities. I said maybe I should do it in Michigan. Mom got really upset. She said wait to do anything until they could find out more about what was going on, especially if the FBI arrested anyone else. I could hear Mom and Dad arguing on the other end of the phone. I got really scared and even more confused. Finally, we agreed I should stay put and call back the next day. Mom said she would tell you about me as soon as it was safe."

"So you called the next day?"

"Yeah, but even though it was Thanksgiving, the FBI had come back to the farm. Mom thought from the questions they asked, if they knew I was alive, they'd arrest me. That's what happened to Jan and two other people in the group. Things changed in that call. Mom and Dad both told me to stay hidden. Dad didn't say too much, but Mom was definite. I felt totally mixed up, like none of it could be real. For the second day in a row, we just agreed that I should stay out of sight."

"But you really hadn't done anything. I mean, you didn't know anything about the bomb, did you?"

"Of course not."

"So you could have come in."

"You mean for a fair trial?" she said with an edge hardening in her voice.

"Yeah, I guess so." A distant, yet very familiar, feeling of defensiveness flashed through me.

"Jim, it was 1970. Don't you remember? Did anything fair ever happen about that war?"

"Look, I'm sorry," I said. "I don't want to make this any harder, but . . ."

"It's not your fault. Please don't apologize. None of it was ever your fault."

Linda sighed deeply then uncurled the leg propped underneath her. She leaned forward in the wicker chair and looked at me intently.

"When I finished talking to my folks, I had completely lost my bearings. I felt trapped in a nightmare. It looked like I was better off dead. My parents wanted me to stay dead. My head just turned in circles, almost like this thing *had* taken my life away, like I was caught in some other life. It took the second night for everything to sink in. By the next morning, I started to think straight, think about what I really had to do. I called home and said I was going to the police."

"So that was on Friday?"

"That's right. I told Mom and Dad I was going to the police in Laurel, and I asked them to go with me. They agreed. I took a motel room to wait for them to pick me up that night. Later in the day, Mom called me. Dad had told her he was going to feed and water the stock before they left. He went in the barn. That's when he shot himself."

A deep, stony silence like the darkest black of the night hung in the room. We both looked down. Neither of us spoke or moved or cried or looked up again for the longest moments of my life.

"When did you find out?" I finally asked.

"Mom called me at the motel about two in the afternoon. She had taken care of the immediate things for Dad and then thought it all through before she called me. We didn't talk very long. I don't think she could. She just said she had already lost her husband to this thing, and she wasn't going to lose her daughter to jail, too. I did what she asked and went back to the commune."

"For how long?"

"Really, not too long at all. Because of the draft, somebody there knew somebody who could set me up with new identification and a social security number. I left Michigan and tried to hide."

"Where?"

"Northern Wisconsin first. I curled my hair and put a red tint in it. I got my first job waitressing in a bar and figured I could just go out at night. You know. In the dark."

"Yeah," I nodded.

"I was so stupid," she said. "Being a young, single, red-headed cocktail waitress wasn't exactly the way to avoid attention. I only stayed in that town a couple of weeks. At first, I never stayed anywhere much more than a year. Eventually, somebody would get too curious about my family or where I grew up or maybe would just want to be better friends. When that happened, I moved on to the next place."

"All over the country?"

"No, just Minnesota, Wisconsin, and Iowa. I would find a small town where I could walk to things. I always thought a bigger place would have too many police who could notice me. I felt the same way about a car. Having a driver's license and owning a car just raised too many questions, made too many records. I decided not to risk it.

Mom always sent me money, more as the years went by. She never said so, but I know she figured out that I couldn't inherit it. She brought me stuff from home and sent news clippings, all kinds of news clippings. I remember when your team won the all-county basketball tournament."

"So your mom came to visit you?"

"Not at first. She thought somebody could find me through her, but after about three years," Linda's voice dropped, "I don't know, maybe it just seemed safer or maybe your fears just wear to the point where they dull. Anyway, she used to visit me four or five times a year. We got to be a family again. Mom just had a daughter named Cindy James."

"God, it's so hard to believe," I said, still sorting through my confusion. "I mean, even the name. Why Cindy James?"

For the first time since the shock of the afternoon's encounter, I could see the faint outline of a smile briefly pass over Linda's face.

"Well, first the guy with ID stuff said to think up a name that sounded like mine, but different. You know, Cindy James, Linda Bray. They have a lot of the same sounds but different initials. Having some of the same sounds makes it easier to learn to answer to the new name."

"So you don't just say 'Who me?'"

"That's part of it, but mostly, it's your name, Jim. James. I picked James for you."

159

"You took my name? You wanted my name, but all these years you never came back?"

"I couldn't."

"But after a while," I said, "who were you hiding from? The FBI must not have been looking for you. You had to know that. After a while, they even let Dean Wilson out of prison."

"You don't understand. It wasn't being arrested that mattered. I wasn't afraid. I was ashamed. My father killed himself because of me."

Linda's voice cracked and she barely managed to complete her last few words before the sobs of uncontrollable tears overcame her. The words she had spoken pressed down in my heart like a huge weight laid upon my chest. I struggled to capture my breath. Slowly, I lifted myself off the sofa and stepped toward Linda. I reached for her hand and gently pulled her up toward me.

"No, Linda," my voice caught in my throat, ". . . no, you're wrong."

She shook with tears as I held her. I searched for words, feeling that none would come. I held her tighter. With the warmth of Linda in my arms, the words crystallized in my mind, the words Linda should hear, the words that only someone who for twenty-five years had revisited his own quiet moments of despair could say.

"You're wrong now about your Dad just like you were wrong then to trust Dean Wilson. But you weren't the only one wrong in 1970. And, you were less wrong than most of us."

She looked up to speak, but I shook my head.

"Let me talk now. You were less wrong, because you were right about the war. The rest of us should have told you that—your mom, your dad, especially me. We didn't tell you, and we pushed you toward what happened in Laurel as much as Dean Wilson pulled you."

I took a deep breath before I continued.

"We all made mistakes. Maybe your father couldn't face a mistake in public, couldn't be wrong in public, but that was his flaw, not yours. It was cruel, what that flaw did to him . . . what it did to you. It cost your dad his life, and, God, it's cost us so much of ours."

Linda laid her head against my chest and held herself against my body. The tears rolled down her face and slowly soaked through my shirt. From those tears, I felt emotions wash away: at first just the shock and anger of today, but gradually, the pain and loneliness more than two decades old.

June 23, 1995

"Jim . . . Jim."

The soft sound of a woman's voice and the gentle touch of a woman's hand on my shoulder stirred me from my sleep. I rolled over and twisted myself out of the curled-up position I had nestled in on Linda's sofa. I could feel Linda sitting next to me on the edge of the cushions, and I opened my eyes to see her gazing down at me.

"It's almost five-thirty, Jim," she said in a hushed voice. "I have to go to work soon."

"Oh, sure," I answered, awakening to a world that still seemed more dream than reality. "I guess you start pretty early."

"Start early. End early." Linda smiled. "It's okay."

The acceptance, tinged with resignation in her voice, told me she had misheard my drowsy words as a commentary on her life.

"Would you like to stop down at the restaurant and get breakfast before you leave?" she asked.

"Is that all right?" I said. "Won't people ask who I am if it looks like we know each other?"

"That doesn't matter. If anybody asks, I'll tell them you are somebody I knew when I was young. When I disappeared, I was hiding from trouble, but for most of these years I've just been hiding from the past." Her voice cracked and she drew a deep breath. "You're the best part of my past. I don't want to hide you."

"Well," I squeezed Linda's hand as I spoke, "I don't usually eat much for breakfast. I'd rather stop down at lunch."

"I thought you said your appointment was supposed to be at ten o'clock."

"I'm not going. I can't go. Twenty-five years ago, I lost you. Now, you're here and you're real. I don't know what happens next, but I do know I can't find you one day and turn around and drive out of this town the next day."

"What about the job?"

"I'll call Tom Conley," I answered. "Other than that, I can't worry about the job right now."

"But you can't sleep here tonight," Linda said without warning.

"I'll get a motel if that's what you want."

"No, I mean you can't sleep on the couch again. I don't think Misty likes sharing her bedroom. You know how selfish cats are. You'll have to be with me."

A smile spread over my face as Linda took her hand and lightly brushed my hair across my forehead. She sat silently for a moment then grew serious again.

"You'll have to learn to call me Cindy. That's who I am now. I can't go backwards. I know that no matter what happens, I'll never be able to go back to West Fork."

"You couldn't go back if you wanted to Li . . . Cindy. It's not there anymore. You know, I never stopped loving you, but I had to stop grieving for you a long time ago. In the last few years, when I've grieved, I've grieved for West Fork. After Bill Dublin died, Margaret closed the store. They stopped playing softball behind the Methodist Church fifteen years ago. The school is closed. The fields are still full of corn, but there aren't half as many farms as there used to be. Even the fences have disappeared. You can't go back to the place where we fell in love, and I can't either. That West Fork doesn't exist anymore."

I saw moisture fill her eyes as she bent down to kiss me.

"At least the love that started there still exists," she whispered. "Maybe that's all that really counts."

I kissed Linda with a passion I had almost forgotten then held onto her hand as she stood up.

"I have to go. I'm sorry. There's some cereal in the cupboard and bagels in the refrigerator. I don't eat much for breakfast, either, but I guess maybe you remember that."

"Hey, don't worry about me," I said in response to a nervousness in Linda's voice that I did not remember.

"Will you come for lunch about eleven-thirty instead of waiting til noon? A little early and I'm not quite so busy."

"Sure." I squeezed her hand one last time. "Eleven-thirty."

My eyes followed Cindy James to the door of her apartment and watched it close behind her as she left for work. The sharp sound of the closing door roused the small black-and-white cat sleeping in one of the wicker chairs.

"It's just you and me, cat," I said.

I looked around the room with a certain amazement that a cat now shared Linda's home. I sensed that the need for companionship during twenty-five years in small apartments brought the once unwelcome feline species into her life. I scanned the room again and wondered just how I would occupy myself for six more hours. I realized that all I truly wanted to do was follow Linda, or Cindy, and never let her out of my sight again. A day earlier, the digital clock on the counter reading 5:35 a.m. would have simply signaled time to go back to sleep. I knew that wouldn't work today. My mind raced with too much excitement to even consider more sleep a possibility.

My eyes drifted from the totally disinterested cat to the portable television on a small wooden stand opposite the sofa. I quickly rejected the notion of giving in to the tube at such an absurdly early hour, but I glanced further down the stand, past the VCR, to a bottom shelf of oversized books. I rolled off the couch and stepped across to the television stand, reaching down for a thick, brown scrapbook with gold-colored trim. I thought of the years that Linda had bounced from small town to small town and could not guess the mementos she might have kept of that life.

Settling back onto the sofa, I placed the heavy volume in my lap and, even before opening it, noticed the bent corners and smooth edge of the cover where the gold trim had completely worn away. I carefully opened the scrapbook wondering how many times Linda must have held it in her hands to cause such wear.

I turned the cover to reveal a plain gray scrapbook page dotted with little squares and odd-sized rectangles of yellowing newspaper clippings. Nothing else adorned the page except for neatly printed dates in Linda's hand accompanying each clipping. The dates began with March 6, 1972 written in the upper left-hand corner of the page. Beneath this notation, the clipping read:

> Plum River Elementary School won the championship
> of the all-county, eighth-grade basketball tournament.
> Plum River defeated Fairwoods Junior High 40 to 39
> in the finals on Saturday. Billy Kimball led the winners
> with 29 points.

I lightly ran my finger across the clipping and thought about that day. I remembered the tall, tall players Fairwoods sent out on the court, Billy Kimball's utter determination, Ronnie Harper's last minute fouls, the despair of watching Billy fumble the ball away as time ran down, and the amazed joy when CJ Martin somehow picked it up and tossed it through the basket. For all these years, I had the memories to carry with me. For all these years, Linda had only a few lines of fading newsprint.

I pored over the clippings, like touring through the pages of my life. There was West Fork: an announcement for the Fourth of July fireworks, resurfacing the highway, Hazel Anderson's retirement, kids home from college or those who made the Dean's List. For two hours, I lost myself in this whisper of West Fork. I thought of the past and I thought of Linda. I looked at the scraps of newspaper so carefully preserved, and I thought about the depth of her feelings for a place so small that the news almost always came in three or four sentence bites and only the obituaries ever claimed more than an inch or two of print.

The power of the past suspended my sense of the present. When I looked back at the clock on the counter, it read 8:20 a.m. I laid the scrapbook down beside me and reached for the phone on the end table. It was time to call Tom Conley. I dialed and waited three rings for an answer.

"Hello."

"Hi, Tom. This is Jim Blair."

"Hi, Mr. Blair. I wasn't sure if you'd call this morning or just come to the office."

"You know, Tom, practically everyone I've ever known in West Fork over the years calls me Jim, but you still say Mr. Blair. Don't you think we should break that habit?"

"Sounds like a good idea. If things work out here, I think I can get used to calling you Jim."

"Tom, that's why I called," I said, wondering with each word what I would say next. "I'm not going to make it today."

"Something come up?" Tom asked. "I hope it's not serious."

"Complicated might be a better word."

"Well, let's figure out another day," Tom offered. "I want to fill this teaching position soon, but this isn't even an official posting, yet. I started by contacting you, so we still have time."

"I appreciate that and I'm proud of what you've accomplished . . ."

"But?" he asked.

"Maybe the best way to put it is that there is a time for everything. West Fork, those years were the time for the kind of job you're talking about. It was great, and I'm glad it meant enough to you that you thought of me for your district. But that time is past for me now."

"Oh, I disagree, Mr. Blair, uh, Jim. Teachers don't lose what you've got."

"No," I answered, "that's not what I mean. I don't want to try to live those West Fork years over again."

"You mean the job up here is too similar? Not a challenge?"

"That's not quite it either." I hesitated then thought back to West Fork. "Tom, you weren't around when the Kimballs had to sell their farm. On the day of the auction, Art and I sat alone for a few minutes. I asked what Billy was going to do, and Art told me Billy was moving away. He said staying would mean living for memories, not for dreams. Art wanted Billy to find some dreams to live for again. That's what I want to do now, Tom. I want a dream to live for, not just a memory."

Epilogue

Kevin McKnight settled into his customary booth for Saturday morning coffee. From my spot behind the restaurant counter, the words *Cindy and Jim's Cafe*, lettered on the front window, formed a perfect arch over his head. Cindy always looked for Kevin. He worked as the naturalist for the Highland Valleys State Park, and Cindy volunteered at the park every Wednesday. I knew her help made a big difference to Kevin in the park's animal sanctuary program.

Cindy had spotted her young friend, too. She carefully looked over the homemade cinnamon rolls then put the largest one on a plate and headed toward Kevin's booth. Kevin ordered a cinnamon roll every Saturday morning, and Cindy always picked out the biggest one in the bakery case for him. I watched them exchange the warm smiles of a friendship that easily bridged the gap of almost forty years in their ages.

Cindy left Kevin his cinnamon roll and moved around the cafe, coffeepot in hand, refilling the cups of the usual Saturday morning idlers. I suspected that Kevin still retained his sense of surprise that the local cafe owner would be such a gifted volunteer assistant. He remarked on a recent Saturday morning that Cindy had exceptional knowledge for a lay person and learned very quickly.

It came as no surprise that Cindy was ahead of Kevin's expectations, and I smiled at the thought of all those times she was way ahead of me. Cindy finished her rounds with the coffeepot and placed it back on the warmer. My smile broadened as I felt her slip her arm around my waist. Kevin McKnight looked over in our direction and nodded to me. On another Saturday morning not long ago, Kevin told me that Cindy and I looked like the happiest couple in the world.

Maybe we are. Maybe we are.

A Note about the Author

Tom McKay is an historian and museum consultant who lives in his hometown of Hampton, Illinois. He worked for more than two decades as Coordinator of the Office of Local History at the State Historical Society of Wisconsin. In 2007, he received a national award from the American Association for State and Local History for an outstanding career of dedicated service to local museums in Iowa and Wisconsin.

Tom has been writing fiction for fifteen years. His short stories have appeared in the *Wapsipinicon Almanac, Vermont Ink, Downstate Story,* the *Wisconsin River Valley Journal,* and the *Out Loud Anthology* series of the Midwest Writing Center in Davenport, Iowa. Small town life has taken him to more pancake breakfasts, household auctions, and softball tournaments than he can count.